# THEY ALSO BURN PEOPLE

MARCOS ANTONIO HERNANDEZ

ISBN-13: 978-1-7348437-8-1 (Paperback edition)

ISBN-13: 978-1-7348437-9-8 (Ebook edition)

"That was but a prelude; where they burn books, they will ultimately burn people as well."

HEINRICH HEINE, *ALMANSOR*, 1821

# CHAPTER ONE

Cortez Vuscar had expected to dread walking up to her in front of the type of people who would care enough about a burning library to stop and stare: the poised, well-dressed individuals in the part of the city where he didn't belong. Surprising himself, however, he was looking forward to it. As soon as more people were there to witness his bravery, he told himself, he would rush out to her and prove his worth once and for all.

The flames crackled high above him. He looked up, and the faint smell of smoke tickled his nostrils. The building was old, having hosted the city's repository of knowledge for over a century. Thick black smoke issued from the highest windows, passing through ancient seals the way water finds its way into a house during the worst rainstorms. It licked the stone masonry surrounding the roof before continuing its ascent into the atmosphere, obscuring the ornate carvings that lined the outside wall. Wisps of thin white smoke curled out from between the exterior columns surrounding the building, evidence of the flames spreading to the lower levels.

The books were burning.

Cortez turned his attention back to the object of his desire from the previous thirteen days: Alara Chel. Her black hair was pulled back from her face, tied in her typical braided ponytail, exposing her mask of horror and sadness. She was his burning obsession, his reason for searching within himself for the courage to be the man she deserved. His primitive instinct awakened with the memory of her hair smelling like roses from the one time he had gotten close enough to experience the fragrance himself. Coming from her, the smell—along with every other enchanting characteristic she possessed—was capable of both inspiring him and rendering him helpless to resist fulfilling her most frivolous wishes. As the fire gained strength high above him, Cortez lost himself in thoughts of her scent; the smoke created by the burning books was the vapor of Alara's pungent floral scent reaching out and brushing his cheek across space and time. Cortez's nose led him into a rose garden waiting for him, which he alone could access.

He couldn't tell if she was crying from where he stood on the side of the building, though he hoped she was. It was his right to dry her tears, hard-fought and well-earned.

The library's entrance was across the street from the vast park that separated the city in two, keeping the struggling, second-class citizens like Cortez away from the domain of the privileged. The library was on the line where property values became prohibitive for most of the city's inhabitants. The wide stone steps that led to the imposing dark wood doors created one final pretentious barrier for those from his part of the city who crossed the park for access to the space, detracting from the humble servitude of the tomes held within. The adjacent park was crosscut with paved paths shaded by dense clusters of trees of uniform height; the trees closest to the street projected their leaves over a path that ran between the park and the street in front of the building, under which onlookers—including Alara—congregated, watching the blaze. The mouths of each person in attendance hung open in astonishment as they witnessed knowledge's destruction, their collective breaths acting as bellows for the growing inferno.

A few individuals were watching the fire from the far side of the street that ran alongside the building where Cortez stood. They called out to him, urging him to get away from the burning library. He turned to them, flashed a smile the way his mother had taught him when spreading the Christian message, and waved. He kept his body as close to the library as possible so Alara wouldn't see him before his grand entrance. Their continued yelling induced a surge of burning panic inside Cortez's chest, the pressure escalating as the heat arrived in his throat. He turned his attention back to Alara. Her eyes were still skyward.

Noticing anything but a burning library that has stood as knowledge's guardian for over a hundred years takes more than yelling.

The distant blaring of sirens from fast-approaching fire trucks pulled Cortez back into the moment and provided the salve for the flames in his chest. He scanned the faces in the crowd around his beloved. Though he wanted more witnesses when he approached her, the few dozen already present were more than he had ever had the courage to stand in front of before. His lack of fear filled him with pride. The previous version of himself, the one before the fire, would have fought himself to abandon the plan, and he had been prepared to storm into battle in the name of love. Standing straight with confidence despite the sharp pain in his ribs—his mother would have been proud—he emerged from the side of the building, heading straight towards where Alara stood beneath the trees' protective leaves.

She didn't notice him. Nobody did. Their eyes were glued to the sky, watching the now-black smoke billowing from between the columns. The sirens were getting closer. Air rushed into the flames behind him through broken windows, creating a peculiar noise of consumption; the fire had emerged from its shell and was taking its first massive breath. Cortez had to say his piece before the firefighters had time to park, set up, and organize a plan of attack against the blaze. Their perimeter would be impenetrable once deployed.

His plan didn't budget time for him to get Alara's attention. The way it had played out in his head, she would see him and be grateful for his arrival. He was the knight in shining armor, she was the rescued princess from the movies. Her gratitude would multiply when she understood what he was prepared to do for her. In the deepest recesses of his heart, he hoped she would rush into his arms and plant a kiss on his lips. He could think of no better scenario for his first. When he was mere steps away, lost in a daydream that would never occur, she turned in his direction, facing him without a trace of recognition.

The truth dawned on Alara when Cortez's path became clear. Her features hardened. "What are you doing here?" she asked, understanding who stood in front of her.

"The library's burning," Cortez replied, as if this simple fact explained his presence as well as if she had asked the same question inside his own home and he replied that he lived there.

"I can't believe it," she said. Her voice carried immeasurable sadness and a hint of resignation.


THE FIRST FIRE truck arrived on the scene, skidding to a stop on the street between the park and the library now behind Cortez. It was in desperate need of a wash, the typical shiny red paint dulled with layers of grime. The attached white ladder had peeling rust spots littering its skin. The fire truck was from the side of the city where Cortez lived with his mother, on the far side of the park; it was the first on-scene because of how the fire stations were distributed throughout the city. It was a shoddy version of the two fire trucks that pulled to a stop soon after. These were red and polished to a high sheen—they were brand new and looked like they belonged in a magazine. As Cortez watched, the two gleaming fire trucks forced the one that had first arrived to back up so they could take the prime position in front of the blaze and receive the lion's share of the glory for saving the great sentinel standing guard against intruders from the far side of the city.

Cortez knew time was running out. He raised his gaze and stared at the fire for a moment, relishing the shared experience with Alara. The crowd, having grown, was large enough, everyone there ready, in his mind, to witness his great emergence from the shadows. He turned to Alara and said, "Remy's in there."

The information caught Alara off guard. She blinked multiple times and shook her head from left to right as she pulled it back, unable or unwilling to accept the news. Part of the confusion came from the way Cortez had shared the information. His tone of voice would have had the same matter-of-fact quality if he had said, "There are books in there." Most of the confusion, however, came from finding out her boyfriend was in the library. Remy Moncard didn't read. He was proud of the fact and owned it, a contorted badge of honor he displayed on his chest. According to him, reading played no part in his plan to further his own station in life. Discipline, charm, and his smile were his winning combination.

"Remy?" Alara repeated when she found her voice.

Cortez's eyes lit up. "Uh-huh," he said with a sweet smile and slight nod. It was a joke to him.

Alara was first repulsed, then grew frantic. "What's he doing in there? How do you know?"

"Relax," Cortez said. He stretched out the beginning of the word, the way it was said on the old sitcoms he used to watch for hours after school while his mother was at work. He adopted the nonchalant air of the show's most charming characters and told her there was nothing to worry about. "There's nothing to worry about. God brought me here for a reason," he said.

"Of course there's something to worry about! Remy's inside a fire!"

"I can save him if you want." His offer was served with a singsong quality, the final word dragged out.

Alara became enraged, her braid hovering above her back, no longer in contact with her body, a cobra preparing to strike. "And what are you going to do?"

Cortez looked at the crowd of people around them; there were plenty of witnesses for his great sacrifice. He imagined they were listening to his conversation with rapt attention without looking out of politeness, their gaze instead drawn to the stage where his production would unfold. Everything Cortez had done for her was coming together just as he had planned. Getting Remy inside the library and starting the fire had given him the chance to prove his devotion.

"I'll go in and get him," Cortez said, imagining he was Jesus accepting his fate for the good of mankind. He stared into her eyes and was shocked to discover disgust where he had expected, and believed he'd earned, admiration.

Part of Alara wondered if Cortez was lying. She knew he didn't like Remy, and wouldn't like any boyfriend of hers, but his absolute conviction in Remy's presence inside the fire was the first time she had heard Cortez speak in a confident, commanding way. The cold power behind his words frightened her. She brushed him aside and walked away, looking for someone who could help her trapped boyfriend. Cortez shuddered at her touch, goosebumps radiating out from the point of their contact.

Pulling himself from his reverie, Cortez grabbed Alara's arm, stopping her before she took her first steps into the street. "I'll be right back," he uttered, his own sudden seriousness evident in his voice. He was silent while he waited for the response to his grand gesture, which he had played on repeat in his mind: the kiss, his first, the one that he knew would bring him into direct contact with God's grace.

Alara froze. As she stood still, Cortez reached a hand up and caressed her cheek, the way he had seen it done in the movies. A crash rang out from inside the library, causing a collective gasp from the onlookers. He imagined it was the crowd in a theater, watching his performance. Cortez was a man possessed by something far greater than himself, and once he realized the kiss wouldn't materialize, he turned his back on the flames of his own passions and prepared himself to rush head-long into the raging inferno inside the library.

Once past Alara, Cortez turned and, walking backwards, said, "If God has put me in a position to help, I can't look the other way."

# CHAPTER TWO

THIRTEEN DAYS before the library fire, Cortez had left the house for work at the same time he did every weekday. He descended the stairs from the seventh floor two at a time with his mother's reminder to have a good day still echoing inside his head. The bright blue backpack hanging from his shoulders carried his daily supplies: a packed lunch in a brown paper bag from his mother, a pencil and notebook that had been blank since its purchase months or years ago, and an assortment of medications he carried with him everywhere. His asthmatic lungs required an inhaler if he overexerted himself or was struck with enough panic to affect his breathing. Blue pills were there to catch him if he fell victim to a panic attack. The white pills helped him whenever he needed an extra dose of courage, like when he was faced with too many social interactions; unbeknownst to him, they were sugar pills not prescribed by a doctor but included in his arsenal by his mother. As a devout Christian woman, she knew the power of belief.

The sun blazed outside his patchwork building, and with it came the smell of baking garbage that flooded Cortez's nostrils as soon as he walked outside. The black trash bags in the alley he passed had been put out the night before and hadn't had enough time in the sun to create enough vapors to account for the stench. Instead, the smell emanated from the concrete and asphalt itself, in the forgotten part of a city where those with less were able to scratch out a corner large enough for them to exist.

Cortez kept his head down as he walked by his neighbors. There had been a time, when he was younger, when he would have greeted those that lived around him, or even looked them in the eye, but after he'd mentioned to his mother that one of them had shown him a handgun, she forbade him to interact with them without her watchful eye there to protect him. He had memorized the cracks in the sidewalk and knew every place water entered the sewer system. He looked forward to walking over the grates that would blow air up from the subway system below but was careful to stay off them in the presence of his guardian, in case she also forbade him to tempt fate.

THE WALK to the ice cream factory was eleven blocks and took him ten minutes. He always arrived five minutes before eight. When the boss arrived, he always found Cortez sitting on the concrete step in front of the door, waiting to be let in. The boss was a surly man by nature, but he started the morning with an inspiring hope that each day would be one worth living before the inevitable small inconvenience ruined his mood and made him look forward to beginning the next.

"Cortez," the boss said when he parked near the factory's entrance. He wore khakis, a yellow polo, and was supported by off-white sneakers that had survived decades of abuse. If Cortez had been more observant, he would have noticed that the different-colored polos his boss wore throughout the week corresponded to the different days. Red on Mondays, to start the week hot. Yellow on Fridays, in anticipation of the weekend and spending time outside in the sun, even though his pale skin turned bright red on the few occasions each year when he followed through with his plan and made it outside. He wore green, blue, and purple polos on the remaining days of the week, according to an internal logic he would take to his grave.

"Morning, sir," Cortez replied. He stood up, waited for the boss to unlock and open the double doors, and followed him inside. After walking through the reception area together—unused save for visits from vendors once a month—the boss turned right and went into the office he still insisted on locking every night, while Cortez turned left and went through a set of swinging double doors and walked onto the factory floor. He liked being the first one there so he could hang his backpack on the third hook from the left, which corresponded to the position of the locker where he kept his coat. Since nobody else paid attention to these things, on days Cortez wasn't the first one to arrive he ran the risk of leaving his belongings disjointed. This would result in a mild sense of dread and panic that sat just below his throat and would last the entire workday, making it difficult to concentrate and requiring many white pills. He had learned long ago that people didn't like their things moved from his hook without their consent, and that consenting to something they didn't understand wasn't an ability anybody he worked with had ever demonstrated.

With his belongings left hanging in their proper place, Cortez turned and went back to the building's entrance. He sat down on the step in front of the door once more to wait for his friend's arrival. Other workers streamed in as the clock approached eight thirty, the time everyone was required in the building so production could begin at nine. Some of his fellow employees shook his hand, some nodded their head in his direction when their eyes met, and one leaned over and patted his back. On some days, Simeon would be waiting for Cortez as soon as he walked back through the front entrance, but this wasn't one of those days.

Cortez was getting anxious by the time Simeon Blough rolled up three minutes before eight thirty. His friend was also Hispanic and had been born without the use of his legs. His black hair was matted on his head, the sides tickling the tops of his ears. As he explained it, showering wasn't something he was concerned with, and what little smell his body generated from sitting in a chair all day was no match for deodorant.

"Hi Cortez," Simeon said, coasting across the final portion of the parking lot. He couldn't wave because both hands were busy monitoring his locomotion, ready to stop on a moment's notice.

"Good morning, Simeon. Long time no see." It was his morning's standard greeting phrase, comforting in its regularity because they saw each other every day during the week.

"Not long enough," Simeon said with a smile, his typical reply. He stopped in front of the step and turned around, his back to Cortez.

Cortez grabbed the handles of his friend's wheelchair, tilted him back, and lifted him over the step. In theory, anybody could perform the minor task, but after Simeon had been left outside in the rain one morning, the boss had told Cortez it was his job from then on. He also helped Simeon get around when they were both inside the factory, a task that left Cortez and Simeon tethered together until the end of each workday. After Simeon was rolled to his locker, he opened it and placed his lunch down on the bottom. According to the chart on the wall near their station, the team would be making orange sorbet pints that day. The pair was responsible for putting lids on the sealed pints. During production, the pair took up stations on opposite sides of the conveyor belt, and each person would be responsible for putting the lids on alternating containers. It was possible for one of them to take over putting lids on every pint if necessary, but they weren't allowed to do it for long because the boss didn't want to risk backing up the entire line. When Simeon's employment had first begun, there was talk about lowering the conveyor belt and allowing Cortez to sit down as well. In the meantime, a wooden platform had been provided where Simeon could apply the brakes to his wheels and be within reach of the belt. It had been over a year since the stopgap measure was instituted.

The pair began getting ready for the morning's production. Cortez grabbed two boxes of orange lids and placed one on each side of the conveyor belt. Then, they both put on hairnets and aprons before Simeon washed his hands and put on gloves. Once Simeon was ready, Cortez got him in position on top of the wooden platform before taking care of his own hands. The pair was ready to go when the boss came to make sure they were in position. Soon after, the conveyor belt started moving. Within minutes, the first pints came down the line.

Simeon and Cortez fell silent as they began putting lid after lid onto the pints of orange sorbet after they had been sealed. It was easy, mindless work. Cortez's skill set was limited, and he was grateful for the job.

"Are you interested in making some extra money?" Simeon asked Cortez with a mischievous glint in his eye once they got into a rhythm.

Cortez knew the struggles his mother had to go through to pay for their home, food, and lives. Every dollar counted, and he gave her every paycheck without questioning where the money went. Still, he was skeptical of his friend's random question because, in his experience, making money was never easy.

"What do you mean?"

"I mean I've got a way for us to get some extra cash in our pockets." Simeon looked around even though the two of them were alone. "I know someone who wants to buy some of those little blue pills you take."

Cortez froze and missed placing lids on two pints that were his responsibility. Simeon covered for him but yelled at him to snap out of it before he became overwhelmed and couldn't cover for his friend.

"It's against the law," Cortez said after they got back into a shared rhythm.

"So? Nobody will find out. It's easy money."

"But I need them."

"So do these guys! They're college students and have big exams coming up. They're stressing out. You can help them. Just say you lost your bottle. New medicine and money in your pocket."

Cortez stayed silent while alternating lid placement with Simeon. After a while, Simeon let out a sigh loud enough to be heard over the low hum of the conveyor belt.

"I'm just trying to help you out, OK?" Simeon said. "We don't have to talk about it."

THEY DIDN'T SAY another word to each other until lunch. Their half hour began when the belt stopped. Cortez took Simeon down from his wooden platform and rolled him to his locker. Simeon took his hairnet, apron, and gloves off during the short trip and put them in his locker. While Simeon grabbed his lunch, Cortez took off his protective clothing and swapped it with his backpack. He then took hold of the handles on Simeon's wheelchair and wheeled him towards the entrance.

"I thought you'd want to eat lunch alone today," Simeon said, upset at being the victim of the silent treatment even though he had created the conditions for the retaliation himself.

"We eat lunch together every day," Cortez said without further justification.

Cortez rolled Simeon off the front step and continued down the street to where two picnic tables were set up beneath a cluster of trees a block away from the factory. The other employees at the factory all went out to eat, or ate their lunch inside the building, so on days it wasn't raining the two friends responsible for lidding pints came to this spot and ate lunch alone. Within minutes, Cortez had spread out his sandwich, small plastic bag of chips, and banana on top of the brown paper bag they'd come in. Simeon drank a can of Coke with a straw and downed three-hours-old taquitos.

By the time Simeon finished, Cortez had polished off his sandwich and chips and was about to work on his banana. He didn't notice Simeon roll backwards so he could get a better look at the street.

"Hey! Over here!" Simeon yelled.

Cortez turned and saw Simeon waving to a group of men down the street. He ate his banana as fast as he could and found himself with a mouthful of fruit when they arrived at the lunch spot.

"This is the guy," Simeon told the three newcomers while pointing at Cortez. They were about the same age as Cortez, hesitant to engage, and carried an air about them that they were on the lookout for what other people said was fashionable instead of creating fashion themselves.

Cortez looked at the group and nodded. He wasn't sure what Simeon was talking about. Everyone looked at Cortez, waiting for him to finish chewing and say something. The last bits of banana went down, and he searched their faces for a sign of what came next.

Simeon took charge. "Show them the pills."

A slap in the face wouldn't have been as surprising as Simeon's command. Cortez didn't move.

"Give us a moment," Simeon said to his three guests. He used his head to gesture for them to walk away. When they were far enough away, he turned to Cortez and unleashed his wrath.

"Look, we both know you need money. Stop being weird about this and get it over with. You can get more pills from the doctor."

"I need those."

"Exactly why the doc will give them to you! These guys are struggling in school. They told me they need to graduate before they can go on their mission trip. You don't want to be the reason they can't spread the word of God, do you?"

Cortez took a good look at the three visitors. They didn't look like any Christians he knew, and something told him they were more interested in curing hangovers on Sunday mornings than going to church. He dashed these thoughts right after they crept into his head, reminding himself judgment was reserved for the Almighty.

"No, I don't," Cortez acquiesced.

"Get them out," Simeon commanded, pointing at Cortez's backpack. Then, he turned to the buyers. "Guys, come on over here." When they got close, he told them the price was ten dollars a pill.

One of the buyers pulled out five twenty-dollar bills and held them out, unsure whether to give the cash to Simeon or Cortez. Simeon reached out his hand and was handed the money.

"Give them ten pills, Cort," Simeon said.

Cortez counted out the pills and handed them to the closest of the three. He looked down into the bottle, shook it, and grew anxious at how much his stockpile had dwindled. After shaking one pill into his palm, he downed it without water, closed the bottle, and closed his eyes.

Police sirens pierced the air. The buyers looked at Simeon, terrified. Simeon called the three buyers rats. One of the alleged college students turned to his companions, told them to run, and all three of them fled.

Inspired by the quick exit of the purchasers, Cortez grabbed his backpack, dropped the bottle into the open center portion, and ran away without zipping it shut, traveling in the direction of the factory. A pang of guilt struck him at having left his trash on the picnic table. It didn't cross his mind that Simeon was a sitting duck until he looked back at their lunch spot from behind the corner of an adjacent building, after taking a puff of his inhaler.

Neither of the two officers bothered giving chase to anyone who fled. Cortez watched as they sauntered up to and engaged with Simeon. The three of them talked for a few minutes before the officers got back into their car and left. Cortez went back to his friend when he was sure the police had gone.

"You left me," Simeon said. He didn't try hiding the anger and disappointment in his voice.

"I wasn't thinking," Cortez replied. "What did they say?"

"They said I should get better friends." Simeon held out four of the twenty-dollar bills. "These are yours," he said.

Cortez accepted the cash. "I thought there were five," Cortez said after counting his cut.

"I get twenty for arranging the deal," Simeon said. "Let's go back to work."

Cortez stuffed the trash from his lunch into his backpack before rolling Simeon back to the factory, where they spent a wordless afternoon lidding pint after pint of orange sorbet.

# CHAPTER THREE

"CORTEZ! WAKE UP!" his mother yelled from the kitchen. She had no way of knowing he had been awake for almost an hour, listening to her make breakfast without any regard for how much noise she was making. Their Sunday breakfast was the one time each week when he ate a meal before leaving the house. Its composition never changed. Two fried eggs, two sausage links, and two tortillas would be waiting on his plate when he came out and began his day. In the event he was still hungry after this portion, he could fill his belly with more tortillas. They were store-bought, came in a bag, and didn't require his mother spending more time cooking than she already had.

"Cortez!" she yelled again.

"I'm up," Cortez grumbled. He didn't have to yell; their apartment was so small they could hear each other at a conversational speaking volume. His mother yelled for the benefit of the neighbors, as if demonstrating the control over her dominion that her son had never threatened. The neighbor women all yelled on different schedules. The Sunday morning slot belonged to his household, Monday through Friday at six Mrs.

Wyatt yelled to her brood to come eat dinner, and Ms. Roberts down the hall screamed around midnight on Friday and Saturday nights whenever she hosted male company. If there was ever a time that every woman happened to yell at the same time, the resulting cracks in the walls could bring their building crashing down.

The white short-sleeved dress shirt he wore each week to church hung in his closet, ironed to sharpen the creases. His blue slacks, also sharpened, lay folded over the bottom portion of the same hanger. The creases his mother had made in the fabric were for the benefit of everyone else who attended their church. According to her belief, the sharper the crease, the more one believed in God, and she did all she could to convince others that her household's level of devotion was on par with the Pope. Cortez put on his clothes, careful to preserve the remnants of the Holy Spirit in the cultivated lines in the fabric. He selected one of his two pairs of blue dress socks and wore them beneath brown loafers that clung to existence from a time before he was born.

Cortez went into the bathroom without greeting his mother, even though he could sense her watching him as he crossed the hallway. After relieving himself of the water stored up overnight and brushing his teeth while paying full attention to keeping his clothes pristine, he combed his hair to the side in the same direction he had every morning since he hit puberty. Combing his hair was the ritual that had the greatest impact on his ability to engage with other people; the act of arranging his hair was the finishing touch on a mask that hid his sinner's nature. Greeting his mother had to wait until he felt ready, but once he left the bathroom, he walked right up to her and planted a kiss on her cheek while she cooked eggs.

"Good morning," he said. The standard greeting.

"Good morning, my son. Are you hungry?" Her standard

reply. She wore a light pink full-length dress and wore a white head covering over her braided hair.

Cortez nodded, and his mother pointed with her spatula to the plate that held the typical Sunday morning meal, just as expected. He grabbed a fork, took the plate, and set it down on the coffee table before taking a seat on the couch. Grease issued from the sausage when he stabbed it, and he leaned over his plate and bit off the end of a link so no grease would fall onto his clothes.

"Wait!" his mother scolded. He set his fork down and sat with his hands folded in his lap.

She finished making her own plate then took it with her before sitting in the reclining chair where she spent every night. Early in the evenings, she watched game shows and the news. As the night progressed, she switched to dramas, the channel and show depending on the night of the week. The tray where she ate her meals was never folded up and put away; instead, she moved it to the side when she wanted to lie back, as sleep crept up on her. With a plate in her left hand, she grabbed the folding tray with her right, setting both down in front of her station before turning her attention back to her son.

Cortez picked up his fork, eager to take another bite of sausage. His pork dreams were dashed when his mother reminded him, in tones harsh enough to chastise sailors, that they needed to pray before they ate, and prayers were more important on Sunday than on any other day of the week. Cortez set the fork down, bowed his head, and folded his hands once more.

"Father, we thank you for this food we are about to eat. May the blessings you have given us extend to everyone we know, and everyone we meet, as we go into the city in your service. Please keep a watchful eye on Cortez as he navigates becoming a man and all the trials and temptations that come along with it.

Teach him that there are people in this world who want to take advantage of his sweet soul, and protect him whenever your path for him puts him in the company of these kind. In your name we pray. Amen."

As the prayer drew to a conclusion, Cortez was sure that his mother knew about him selling pills at lunch on Friday. Did she know that Simeon had forced him? Had Simeon told the police about him, and had they contacted her? As the possibilities of his discovery swirled through his guilty mind, he missed saying "Amen" in time with his mother, and he said it well after she was done speaking.

She began her meal by rearranging the food on her plate using her fork, taking measure of the most appetizing bite, similar to the way birds peck at a crust of bread a few times before flying off with the entire piece in their mouth. Once she determined the moment's perfect bite, she placed it into her mouth and chewed a set number of times, a number only she knew and that varied depending on the food.

Cortez dove into his food with a hunger strengthened by fear. By focusing on his meal, he hoped to forget his mother's prescient prayer. He was done with breakfast well before his mother, and he had to wait for her to finish chewing every last bird bite before she informed him it was time they left for church.


THE CHURCH WAS a fifteen-minute walk from their apartment. They walked together, with personal Bibles beneath their arms, at a slower pace than Cortez would have walked alone. His mother wasn't too old to walk fast; she was one of those people who took great care when they walked to make sure anyone looking wouldn't think she was in a hurry. Their congregation met in the auditorium of a public middle school. The prevailing sentiment about their choice of space was that God could be worshipped anywhere, and they could be more effective in their evangelism if they weren't viewed as having an ornate, imposing structure looking down on nonbelievers. In reality, their financials had never allowed them to consider meeting anywhere but the large spaces of public buildings, a fact the church elders took great care to spin in a way that made their situation favorable.

After church, the majority of the afternoon would be spent out on the streets, trying to spread the word of God to anyone who would listen. Each week's service spent a large portion of the time extolling the virtues of converting sinners, and the members of the church each accepted their holy mission to find the most converts. Over the years, spreading God's word had become an unspoken competition among the parishioners. Every one of them belonged to a tree that traced its roots back to the member who was responsible for the chain of conversions. A hierarchy had formed; Cortez and his mother occupied its bottom rungs.

Cortez had yet to convince a single person to join him on Sundays. He'd had hopes for Simeon when they first met, but after weeks of excuses Cortez had dropped the subject and was still waiting for the right time to bring it up once more. His mother was on the same step of the church's unspoken ladder as him—the lone soul she had brought into the church for saving was Cortez.

The church service faded to the background as Cortez lost himself in daydreams of finding a rich seam of precious souls he could mine. His body carried him through the familiar motions of the service: the hymns, the communion, the congregation's vocalized responses to the priest's prayers. After the final "Amen" was said, he shook himself out of his stupor and prepared to stand next to his mother while she made the rounds of her weekly small talk. The women and men stood apart;

Cortez never joined the other men. The congregation's children split into two groups: the younger children played together in the hallway, and the teenagers sat in the empty, still-warm chairs. Cortez was the only child who never left his parent's side.

The reunions lasted half an hour and ended when the priest, his robe removed and now sporting a light blue shirt and navy pants, announced the arrival of lunch. After the sandwiches were wolfed down, the priest asked his flock if they were ready to go fishing, the preferred metaphor for finding new church members. A more enthusiastic group might have responded with a loud collective "Yes!," but the members of Cortez's church murmured their agreement. He didn't repeat the question, wanting to avoid another lackluster response and knowing his inability to generate more excitement himself.

"Now remember, you have all the tools you need in your hand," the priest said, holding up the Bible. "We want to spread the Lord's message and find more people to join us in worship. Good luck, everyone, and God bless!"

With that blessing, the members of the congregation were released. A wave of excitement washed over Cortez when he walked outside, a combination of no longer being trapped indoors, the removal of the social yoke he'd never quite figured out how to carry, and the promise of winning the respect of the rest of the group through his evangelism. Although he had yet to convince anyone to join him on Sundays, each week he was convinced this would be the one when his luck would change. His mother had always told him he was destined for greatness and that once his father heard about what a fine young man Cortez had become, he'd rejoin their little family. Evangelism was his chance to fulfill his destiny and make his parents proud. It was also when his mother allowed him to leave her side, and he was determined to show his worth by completing his holy task alone.

It was no secret that some of the members of the congregation went home instead of looking for souls to save. These people stayed for the free lunch after worship but were never seen in the streets. Cortez saw their absence as an opportunity: he had less competition for glory. Together with his mother, he walked for blocks in the opposite direction of their home, into new parts of the decaying city. As they passed beneath aboveground railway tracks, Cortez announced he was turning left into a part of the city he had flagged as a potential fishing spot the week before.

"Be careful, and good luck," his mother said. "I'm going to a restaurant this way to see if I can talk to people leaving lunch." She pointed in the direction they were already walking.

"See you soon," Cortez said. He took a white pill for courage.

WHERE OTHER PEOPLE saw spoilage in the abandoned storefronts on the road that ran alongside the tracks, Cortez saw opportunity. He got the feeling he was walking the right path, as if destiny herself had made the decision for him long ago and he had discovered her plan for him. Every nook had the remnants of a homeless person's presence from the night before, and every corner had groups milling about without purpose—none of them were the ones he was looking for. Block after block passed by while he walked, searching for destiny's next sign.

He passed a woman wearing a skirt and halter top. Her clothes looked like they had been worn for days, stretched out and looser-fitting than designed, and parts of her unkempt hair stuck out at odd angles. "Are you lonely, honey?" she called out to him.

Cortez would have ignored her if he wasn't infused with the Holy Spirit. Instead, he asked if she had friends.

"I do, they're right over there." She pointed across the street, to another street that ran to the left.

"I want to talk to them," Cortez said. An excitement built in his stomach, a certainty that he was on the right track.

"We'll do more than talking," the woman said, trying her best to force her dull eyes to twinkle. "Let's go."

Cortez followed her as she led the way, his Bible tucked under his arm. He didn't notice the confused looks of people that drove past with their windows rolled up. The woman was aged beyond her years. She wasn't much older than him, but her body spent more time healing the bruises and sores on her arms and legs than fighting back the wrinkles on her face. She walked tall, having made peace with her position in life. They found the woman's four friends standing in an alley.

"What do you have in mind?" the messy-haired woman asked. She said it loud enough for her friends to hear.

When their attention turned to him, Cortez knew the time had come to face the most difficult part of his mission. Whatever uncertainty he had harbored about talking to the group was suppressed by the certainty that he was a messenger from God, with help from his pill. "I'm here today to speak with you about our Lord and Savior Jesus Christ." These were the exact words the church had drilled into his head over the years about how best to begin the conversion.

In unison, the women rolled their eyes and shook their heads, each one a marionette controlled by the same set of puppet master's strings.

"Why'd you bring him over here," the oldest-looking woman in the group said.

Cortez ignored their reaction. He opened his Bible using the bookmark he had inserted for this moment. He began to read, "It is not the healthy who need a doctor, but the sick. I have not come to call the righteous, but the sinners." He closed the book, keeping his thumb inserted to the spot in case the women wanted to hear more. He looked at them with an expectant smile on his face.

The smile disappeared when he saw the anger in their eyes. "So you're calling us sinners? Like we don't know that already?" the woman who had brought him said. She pushed him back in the direction of the street. "Do you think you're better than us? What the hell is the matter with you?" she demanded to know.

A car door opened across the street and a large man got out. He stood tall, his gold rings and necklace sparkling in the sunlight. "Hey!" he yelled out. "Quit bothering the girls!"

Cortez looked at him, confused. Didn't these people realize he was there to save them? "I'm not bothering them," he said.

The man walked right up to Cortez and grabbed him by his shirt's collar, wrinkling it and driving out the Holy Spirit contained within. "Get out of here," he snarled. Crumbs littered the collar of his black shirt.

Memories of Daniel in the lions' den gave Cortez strength. "Our church meets at ten on Sunday mornings. Would you like the address?"

"No, I don't want the damned address!" the imposing man said. "What part of get out of here do you not understand?"

Cortez was convinced he had found the big fish he had been searching for. If he could convince this man to join him in worship, the others might follow. He was about to try again when he heard his mother yell out from the direction he had come.

"Cortez! It's time to go home!" she said.

Everyone turned to watch the woman fly down the street, carried by angels. Her white head covering trailed in the breeze as she approached, and it settled on her back when she stopped.

"Good afternoon, everyone," she said, with a polite nod to the bejeweled man. "Thank you for finding my son." She grabbed Cortez's arm and pried him loose from the man's iron grip. "Let's go," she said.

"But these people need God," Cortez pleaded.

The women all laughed. The man, still angry, didn't find it funny.

"And you'll meet God soon enough if we don't go home," his mother said, her tone firm. Cortez knew not to push back when she spoke this way.

"God bless," his mother said as a farewell.

The women repeated the phrase, sneering, as they waved goodbye.

"What are you doing here? I was going to get them to come to church next week," Cortez said to his mother as they started the trip home.

"I followed you, to make sure something like this didn't happen." She had calmed down now that her son was no longer in danger, though her shoulders still rose with each of her deep breaths.

They walked in silence for a long time before Cortez spoke again. "They need our help. They need *God's* help."

Cortez's mother stopped, grabbed Cortez's shoulders, and looked into his eyes. "The Church doesn't want those kinds of people."

# CHAPTER FOUR

The boss arrived at work Monday morning wearing his red polo. He waved from inside his car when he saw Cortez waiting in front of the factory's entrance. It was raining, a light drizzle that made one wonder whether it was worth it to go through the hassle of carrying an umbrella. Cortez had opted for a navy-blue rain jacket to combat the elements. He had learned to keep his backpack beneath the jacket years ago on his trips to school, but he didn't account for the lack of coverage when he sat down on the wet concrete step. That was why he found himself with a wet bottom while watching his boss take a few deep breaths before getting out of the car.

"I swear people don't know how to drive," the boss said.

"It's the rain," Cortez replied. It was something he heard people say. He didn't have his license and had never driven a car. People in the city didn't have the same pressure to drive, since everything one might need was within walking distance. In the event someone needed to travel farther distances, they could always take public transportation: ancient buses and rickety underground trains crossed the city at all hours of the day and night. The boss drove a car because he commuted into the city from beyond the outskirts. Even though his car was an older model, the fact that he drove at all provided the elevated status he needed to look down on those around him.

"And the day started so well too."

Cortez stood up, giving his boss access to the main door. Once inside, he took off his rain jacket in order to take off his backpack and hang it up in its proper location, then he put the jacket back on before going back outside to wait for Simeon. The sky couldn't decide whether it was done raining or not. Its color didn't change, but pockets of clear weather emerged, on one occasion leaving Cortez untouched while droplets of water hit the puddles around him. He didn't have to wait long for Simeon to roll up to the factory. As soon as Cortez spotted his friend passing the neighboring building, he walked forward so he could push the wheelchair the remaining distance, which would keep his friend's hands from touching more rainwater on the wheels.

"Morning, Cort," Simeon said. He was cheerful in a way Cortez had witnessed a handful of times before. His hair was matted against his head, this time because he didn't have an umbrella or a rain jacket. The shoulders of his shirt were soaked through, the moisture fading away towards the still-dry parts around his stomach. Sunken eyes surrounded by dark circles crinkled at the edges when he smiled, as Cortez hurried to get behind his wheelchair and push him the remaining distance.

"How was your weekend?" Simeon asked.

"It was good. Went to church," Cortez replied. He turned the wheelchair around and pulled the wheels over the concrete step with a grunt.

"Of course you did," Simeon said. He continued when Cortez didn't say anything more. "My weekend was good too. Sat around mostly." Simeon turned around and looked at

Cortez out of the corner of his eye with his mouth hanging open.

"That's nice," Cortez said, wheeling his friend towards the factory floor.

"Nothing? You get it, don't you? I'm *always* sitting!" Simeon said.

Cortez thought for a moment, still didn't understand, then let a chuckle escape his lips because something in the way Simeon looked at him informed him it was the right thing to do.

Simeon shook his head, a switch flipped, and he became irritated. "My jokes are wasted on you. You don't appreciate anything."

Cortez ignored Simeon's erratic mood and took a look at the board with the day's production schedule. They were in for a busy one. There were two different flavors being made in the morning, and three in the afternoon. He had to get two different boxes of lids on each side of the conveyor belt before morning production started, and it would be helpful if he located the lids they would need that afternoon. It was a good thing Simeon had arrived a little earlier than normal. There wasn't much Simeon could do while Cortez gathered boxes from where they were stored, carried them to their station, and took care to arrange them within Simeon's reach.

The pair were on their respective sides of the conveyor belt when production began. The morning was dedicated to water-based flavors because it was easier to transition to milk-based flavors than going from milk to water. Raspberry sorbet got red lids, and they worked for an hour before the conveyor belt stopped. When it started back up again, mango was coming down the line. Cortez hadn't been paying attention and began placing red lids on each pint, and when Simeon pointed it out, he had to hurry and switch the few mistakes he'd made with the necessary pale orange lids while Simeon lidded the oncoming pints alone. The team making the pints was working faster than normal in order to get the orders completed, leaving both Cortez and Simeon so busy that they were slightly out of breath, with no air left to chat.

They welcomed the arrival of their lunch break. Simeon had never dried out; the rain had been replaced with sweat, his hair still matted to his head. Instead of the moisture originating from his shoulders, it now spread out from his armpits. Cortez ripped off his hairnet and plastic gloves. His hands welcomed the cool air of the air-conditioned room after being trapped and unable to breathe. The pair caught each other's eye, and Simeon said, "That was a lot."

"Busy day," Cortez replied. "And there are three this afternoon."

"Bet you're looking forward to lunch," Simeon said.

"Of course. I think I have a sandwich today."

"Cort. You always have a sandwich."

"That's very true." Cortez walked to Simeon's side of the belt, undid the brakes on his wheels, and rolled him off the wooden block. He left Simeon while he went back and moved the boxes they'd used in the morning away from their station, so he had space to bring the new boxes in after lunch. Then he rolled Simeon back to where they kept their belongings. While there, he took a puff from his inhaler before throwing his backpack over his shoulders and turning to his friend. Simeon hadn't taken his lunch from his locker. In fact, he hadn't moved from the spot where Cortez left him.

"I'm going to skip lunch today," Simeon said, looking disappointed. "I need to talk to the boss."

This had never happened before, and Cortez didn't know how to feel. He had never considered whether he liked their shared lunch time, but it was a consistent part of his day, a sure thing he knew was coming and had navigated many times before. He wasn't even sure he would be able to eat in their normal spot—it depended on if the sky had decided to call it quits after depositing enough water for the day. Would his sandwich taste the same when eaten alone again after so long with Simeon for company?

"Do you want me to roll you to the boss's office?" Cortez asked.

"No, I think I can manage." Simeon rolled himself away, and Cortez realized he was still wearing his plastic gloves.

THE SUN WAS SHINING when Cortez went outside. It was bright and hot enough to dry off the world while he had been working inside, and if he hadn't been in the morning rain, he wouldn't have believed the bad weather had passed through. Black birds were perched on the wires that ran between telephone poles, so many that they covered the span and their friends were left flying around looking for somewhere to land. On the way to his picnic table, he thought he saw someone in the driver's seat of an unmarked police car staring at him through the windshield. He remembered his mother's wisdom, told to him after being caught hiding candy he had been forbidden from gathering on Halloween: guilty people act guilty. Acting innocent wasn't hard—Simeon had sold the drugs, against his wishes—but he imagined the cops might want to talk to him if they recognized him as one of the people who had run the previous Friday. Finding strength in his most innocent thoughts, he walked towards the picnic table with his head held high, sat down, and took out his lunch, then began to eat.

Nobody approached him during his meal or while he sat waiting for the end of his lunch break. He forgot Simeon wasn't with him. They ate in silence most days, each lost in their own thoughts. The flames of their conversations never burned bright;

instead, they were the coals at the bottom of a hot fire, always ready to ignite if given fuel. Cortez was comfortable alone, and, despite his misgivings, his lunch that day had tasted the same as it always did. He never figured out that the part of his routine that was most soothing to his soul was getting outside and sitting among the trees. They watched over him with their steady gaze, unaffected by the day-to-day happenings of the people who walked among their trunks, growing and marking periods of time in a way not perceivable by humans. The trees, the consistent friends he never knew he had, kept Cortez company while he ate.

Cortez gathered his lunch's trash into his backpack and went back to the factory. Simeon had positioned himself in front of his own locker and sat with the evidence of his eaten lunch on his lap. He was finishing his Coke when Cortez arrived and didn't turn around when Cortez hung his backpack back in its usual spot. Instead, he stared into his open locker, as if hoping to find the answer to the meaning of life in the emptiness of the locker's dark interior.

"How was lunch?" Cortez asked.

Simeon pulled his head back, blinking multiple times in rapid succession, as he was pulled from his reverie. He turned to look at Cortez. "It was good," he said. He drank the rest of his beverage in one long pull on the straw, then placed it on his lap with the rest of the trash, rolled to the trash can, and deposited everything from his lap inside.

Cortez watched his friend through the stifling air of being ignored. "Everything all right with the boss?" Cortez said.

"Everything's fine." Simeon said. He turned his wheelchair around to face Cortez. "Don't you have to get ready for production?"

Cortez nodded and hurried off to gather the lids the pair would need for the afternoon without a second thought about

Simeon's attitude. He had been raised to believe that if someone was upset, the best thing to do was whatever they expected for as long as necessary in order to get back in their good graces. One time, his mother had been upset with him for an entire week. Cortez never knew that the pressure of being his mother, caring for him day after day, year after year, had gotten to her. All he knew was that the house needed cleaning and the mail needed gathering, and he managed to feed himself while she stayed in her bedroom and ignored him. She emerged from her withdrawal without mentioning her disappearance, and this was how he learned that acts of service would lead to a return to normalcy, as long as he could hold up his end of the bargain.

He took the four boxes of the two types of lids they'd used in the morning, now far lighter than before, and carried them into the warehouse in four trips. Simeon was still near his locker when Cortez looked at the board and determined which color lids they would need for the afternoon. Six trips were needed to bring the lids for the three flavors they were making—two boxes of each color, one for each side of the conveyor belt. By the time everything was arranged for them to begin, Simeon was already next to the wooden block with his hairnet, gloves, and apron on, waiting for Cortez to put him on the riser. Cortez hurried to put on his own gear and tied his apron as he went over to Simeon and helped him into position before putting on his gloves.

They were standing in silence when the conveyor belt began moving, and they performed their duties in silence. Simeon didn't acknowledge Cortez during the color change, when Cortez moved the box of white lids for vanilla out of the way and brought the brown ones for chocolate chip into Simeon's reach. The final switch of the afternoon involved bringing the green lids close for the mint chocolate chip, and they continued working for the rest of the afternoon, finishing a half hour past the normal end of their workday.

. . .

SIMEON RIPPED his hairnet and gloves off when the conveyor belt stopped for the final time and waited for Cortez to help him off the riser. He rolled away at the first chance he got. Cortez was left alone while he packed up the boxes and carried them to the warehouse. During his second trip, the boss stopped him on his way back to the factory floor and asked Cortez to come to his office before he left for the day. Cortez nodded, then went back to grab another box and return it to the warehouse. While carrying it, he saw Simeon rolling himself towards the front door. He called out to Simeon, telling him to wait.

"I'll help you down the step, just wait for me to put the lids away," he said to the back of his friend's head.

When Simeon ignored him, Cortez set the box down and hurried to catch up. They were in the reception area at the front of the factory, with the front door across the room. "Hold on, let me help," Cortez said, reaching out and grabbing one of the wheelchair's handles.

Simeon twisted his torso as if Cortez had grabbed his shoulder and needed to be shaken off. "I don't need you to do everything for me," Simeon spat out. "There are other people here, you know."

Cortez looked around. He didn't point out that they were alone as he took his hand off the wheelchair. "I'll see you tomorrow then?" Cortez said, his voice rising as he came to the end of the phrase, implying a question.

"Whatever," Simeon said.

Cortez watched as his friend wheeled away, opened the front door, and went through it. He waited to hear if there was a commotion past the front door, but all was silent. He took a deep breath then returned to carrying boxes. He arrived at his boss's office with a sheen of sweat covering his face and a fresh puff from his inhaler in his lungs.

"You wanted to see me?" he said after sticking his head through the door. The boss was leaning back in his chair, his head back, staring at the ceiling, looking like he hadn't moved in a while. His desk was cleared of paper, the day's work already filed away to be dealt with tomorrow.

"Come in," the boss said. He didn't offer Cortez a seat.

Cortez shut the door behind him and turned to face his boss. His heart was pounding. Years of conditioning by the public school system had taught him to fear one-on-one interactions with men in power, and he struggled to focus when every fiber of his being screamed to do whatever was necessary to remove himself from the situation.

"I'll make this quick," the boss began. "Today was your last day working here."

Those words took the air from the room, leaving Cortez breathless and suffocating. His vision narrowed, and he realized too late that the pills he had for these situations were in the backpack still hanging on his hook. He scanned his boss's face, searching for a hint of sympathy. The Church had taught him the power of prayer to bring about salvation but had never mentioned how someone could save themselves if they forgot every prayer they'd ever been taught.

"Are you going to say anything?" the boss said.

Cortez stared at his boss. He had a hard face lined by years of imposing his will on people whom he had decided were not, and would never be, good enough. His too-dark hair, dyed for years, was beginning to show hints of gray at the roots.

This wasn't the first time the boss had had to give someone their walking papers, but it was the first time the recipient hadn't said a word. The first thing others had inquired about was why, which was followed either by a fierce defense and a promise to change or a proclamation that the job wasn't what they wanted in the first place and they'd be happy to leave. Cortez reminded the boss of when he had visited his uncle's farm as a boy—times he thought he'd forgotten. Years ago, he had tried to save the calves reared for veal as they were led to slaughter. His uncle had put one hand over his shoulder and squeezed tight as they watched the animals march past at a relaxed pace. In a show of compassion, his uncle didn't make him watch their ultimate demise. The creature in front of him now, just told about his termination, didn't know enough to fight for his life.

The boss looked past Cortez, sure that not looking at him would be the best way to fight the urge to save him. "A tip for your next job: don't sell drugs on company time. Simeon told me all about the way you let him take the fall when the police arrived. What you do on your own time is nobody's business, but during lunch? That's not smart." He forced himself to look at Cortez, not knowing that this act of bravery paled in comparison to the courage it took for Cortez to not run away.

Cortez looked down at his shoes. He knew, without ever being able to put it into words, to do what those with power wanted until he was back on their good side. Don't fight back; it could make the situation worse. Acquiesce until you're forgiven. Worship until your salvation. He managed to say, "I'm sorry," the two words he kept tucked away for every time he faced someone else's disappointment, before turning and leaving the boss alone in his office.

# CHAPTER FIVE

THE WALK back to his apartment was spent waiting for the blue pill to work its magic. Cortez had first been given the pills years ago, the latest in a string of medications prescribed by various doctors all attempting to aid him with conforming to society. There was no telling when he would need them. Weeks would go by without a single thought of the little blue pill that would make human interactions less stressful, then a trigger would begin a series of days where nothing was possible without their support. He was told they weren't habit-forming, but his mother could always tell when he had been on them on a consistent basis for too long; she would beg him to try existing without their help. She claimed it took away his spark, his unique ability to light up the world, the certainty of this ability bestowed upon her by angels the moment he left her womb.

The sun was setting. In the blocks between the factory and Cortez's home, rats were waking up after sleeping all day inside hidden places the best exterminators could never find. The people whose waste products sponsored the rodents' existence congregated on porches, steps, and street corners. Whether they sat or stood depended on their years of hard living. Older people sat with their contemporaries, talking about the past and hoping that each word would prevent the decay of their memories. On the rare occasions Cortez's mother joined in the evening outdoor community, always with Cortez by her side, he was able to glimpse each person's idealized version of heaven. His mother's never included him. The younger people stood, always ready to greet a newcomer or go off on an adventure to a new gathering place. Cortez never talked to the other people his age in the neighborhood, even though he had attended school with all of them. He had trouble remembering their names even when he saw them every day, and now that they weren't in school together anymore, their faces were hazy reminders of memories from a time he wished to be forgotten. It was a curse familiar to all who can't relax enough in their own skin to enjoy the company of anyone else.

Normalcy returned by the time he got to his building's block. The dread of confrontation constricting his heart had passed, allowing blood to flow back to his arms, legs, and lungs. The fresh air had helped. His hand reached out for the few trees he passed, lone sentinels at random intervals along the street, and the feel of the last one's bark grazing his hand reminded his nervous system that he was close to home. The awareness of his proximity to his room brought a fresh surge of anxiety, stemming from his mother's constant proclamations of his untapped greatness. He had lost his job and didn't know how to keep from disappointing her with the news. The feeling of inadequacy was familiar. It had occurred often when he was still in school and would come home with grades in the bottom third of the class. It wasn't for lack of trying—he was afraid to disappoint even before assignments began, which gave him the strength to use every ounce of his meager resources, but still his results would come up short. He wondered how he should break the news to his mother, whether he should include Simeon's deception. She had met Simeon a few times and liked him, and Cortez believed that she wouldn't see the sinner's heart of his former coworker and would take offense to laying the blame on someone without the use of their legs.

A headache was on the horizon. He got them whenever dread overwhelmed him, as if his head couldn't sink any lower and his neck wasn't able to fulfill its responsibility without causing pain further up the chain. The white pills helped, and he took one as the back of his eyes started to ache during his climb to the seventh floor—the elevator always smelled like a flatulent dog had come in from the rain and slept there overnight. To Cortez, taking the stairs was his chance to thank the Lord for providing him with two good legs, one more chance to communicate with a higher power each day. When the first six floors were left behind, he stood preparing himself in the stairwell behind the door that led into the seventh floor's hallway. He never lied to his mother, and he didn't have any intention of doing so, but he decided to keep the information about the end of his workday to himself unless she asked about his employment status. If he divulged he had a headache, he might be able to get away with short replies to any question she asked.

Somehow, Cortez discovered a floating plank of optimism and clung to it for dear life. Even though his mother had found him both jobs he'd ever had, starting the next day, he could go out and find a new one. The sting of having lost the job at the ice cream factory would hurt her much less if she knew his employment had already been addressed.

As soon as he walked into their home, Cortez could tell his mother was confronting another depressive episode. Trash had been left on the counter right next to the garbage can, uneaten food still on a plate on the tray next to her recliner. The television was on mute, a telenovela where the actress's mouth was wide open in surprise and shock after a soundless revelation by a man dressed in all black. He knew his mother was in her bedroom, lying on her bed, in all likelihood staring at the ceiling and hoping a fly would walk across an eyeball. Even if she acknowledged his existence, there was no way she was making him dinner that evening. Cortez set his backpack down on the couch and began cleaning up after her, hoping she'd appreciate what he'd done when she returned from the gloom. He discovered that the oven was still on, and when he looked inside he found a blackened pizza. He took it out and the oven door shut with a loud slam.

"Did you see I made you dinner?" his mother called out from the other room, her voice carrying over the sea of her sadness.

"I did. Thank you," Cortez said, before tossing the burnt pizza in the trash. There was no time to worry about having lost his job earlier that day, of being accused of selling drugs. It was his mother's time of need, and he was called into the same supportive role he'd filled since the first time it had happened mere days after she'd given birth to him. As a days-old newborn, he had figured out how to feed himself, go to the bathroom, and fall asleep alone. The energy it took had left his brain without the foundation it needed to thrive, resulting in his stunted mental abilities after a stellar first few days of life that suggested he would end up as one of humankind's shining examples of what was possible. He had faith, as he had throughout every moment of his mother's previous depressive episodes, that as long as he provided value in her time of need, he would be in her good graces when things went back to normal.

Cortez spent the evening eating canned beans, stale tortillas, and scoops of peanut butter, not knowing if the tears making his food salty fell because of the telenovela still on the television or because of the perceived hopelessness of his situation. Money was an ever-present concern for his household, a specter that stood next to the grim reaper just outside their door, each waiting for their time to collect. He had just given her his prior month's earnings a week before. He wondered what would happen with the wages he'd earned in the week and one day he'd worked at the ice cream factory since then. As much as he knew they needed the money, he also didn't want to ever come into contact with his former boss again. Doing so was an invitation for an avalanche of shame to come down from above. Plus, he couldn't imagine seeing Simeon ever again. A small pit of anger tried to sprout deep in his stomach, but Cortez's desire to avoid confrontation burned stronger than his desire for revenge, incinerating the pit and its pale green shoot before it could take root.

HE AWOKE on the couch during the middle of the night, cleared the coffee table, and turned off the television, then went to his room after setting his alarm. His mother was still asleep when he awoke the next morning at the work week's usual time. The hotel where she worked was aware of her periodic need to sequester herself, and the other maids worked together to make sure the rooms she was responsible for were kept clean. In turn, she never took vacations, making it a point to pick up the slack whenever one of her coworkers wanted to take time off. Her son's termination, evidenced by his changed routine, was the last thing she needed to discover while she was bedridden. Cortez made a peanut butter and jelly sandwich that smeared its contents on the inside of the plastic sandwich bag because he could never quite figure out how to keep the fillings confined to the bread. He drank a glass of water while packing the rest of his standard lunch, placing the too-ripe banana covered with brown spots at the top of the paper bag. The paper bag got placed into his backpack, and he took one last look at the apartment before he left, making sure it was clean. His mother deserved a spotless home if she did manage to pull herself out of bed.

Cortez didn't know where to go in his search for work. He started in the direction of the factory, then stopped on the corner before crossing the street a block from his apartment. The only other place he had gone during the previous months was the church. Craving the familiar, he walked towards the place of worship. He forgot it was used as a school during the week until he arrived, and he stood outside the familiar building with unfamiliar occupants unsure of his next move. He paced back and forth in front of the entrance with slow, unhurried steps while he thought. As the minutes passed, he wondered if there was a job for him at the school. He knew he couldn't be a teacher, since school had never been easy for him in the first place and he didn't want to pass along his struggles to the future generation. If there were any boxes that needed moving he'd be the man for the job, but a school wasn't a warehouse, and he dashed the idea of their need for those services as soon as the inspiration arrived. He knew someone had to clean the place, and while he weighed the chances of their need for a janitor, the front door opened and the priest strolled out with a box in his hands.

"Hello, sir," Cortez said when the priest descended the final step.

"Hello," the priest said. He didn't recognize Cortez, having only seen him on Sundays, and even then the young man was always in his mother's shadow. The priest's eyes were close-set, and a pair of thin wire-framed glasses rested too far down the bridge of his nose.

Cortez could tell the priest wasn't going to stop and talk to him, but he couldn't resist the compulsion to confess. "I wasn't able to convince anyone to come to service next week," he said, divulging yet another of his failures.

A flash of recognition passed over the priest's face. "Ah, yes. That's why the Lord has taught us patience," he said. His voice had changed, going from a disinterested citizen to a knowing elder, a switch more prominent than if he had changed into his robe with a snap. He looked down at the box in his hands and blushed. "I don't normally come here during the week," he added.

Cortez took the statement as a question. "Me neither," Cortez said. The priest waited for Cortez to continue. "I had to pick up something down the street for work." The grip of panic set into Cortez's stomach when he realized he had lied to the priest. He looked up at the clouds, certain lightning was about to strike him down.

"Something for work," the priest echoed, his voice trailing off. He looked down at the box again. "Me too, just grabbing some things I need," he said. He adjusted the weight of the box, his thin arms stretched to their full length to accommodate its size. The two of them stood still for a moment, each unwilling to share more information. "I'd better get going," the priest said.

"Me too," Cortez replied. "Lots to do!" He had adopted the getaway phrase years ago, when he first understood that people expected everyone else to be busy. It was his way of getting out of conversations while still being friendly. In his worst daydreams, the people he walked away from would continue judging him long after he left, going over his peculiarity in their minds. He would die without ever realizing that people have far more important things to do than scrutinize the actions of a somber, forgettable individual.

Before the priest could get too far away, Cortez yelled to his back. "See you Sunday!" The priest didn't even nod.

. . .

CORTEZ FORGOT his plan to inquire about working at the school, instead wanting to leave the space and the memories of the interaction behind. He started walking in the opposite direction of the priest and soon found himself staring at a vast park at the edge of his side of town. It appeared out of nowhere; one minute, he was between dilapidated housing, and the next he was staring at green that loomed over everything for blocks to the left and right. There were tree-lined paths hosting the occasional walker, the leaves above them swaying in the breeze. Through the trunks he could see a wide-open space where a group of mothers, each with a stroller, stood talking. The few clouds overhead posed no threat of rain and let intermittent rays of sunlight through their cover. He had never had any reason, or opportunity, to travel so far from home before, so the park had been unknown to him before that revelation. The trees called out to him, begging him to crash his boat among their shores. He listened to their song, stepping one foot into the street, and was pulled from his enchantment by the honk of a horn and the whoosh of air as a vehicle sped past.

He lost all track of time as he strolled through the trees. It could have been minutes, it could have been days; all Cortez knew was that he was among friends. The path he followed took him straight across the green space in the center of the city, and by the time he regained his senses he stood staring at a different city altogether, with the library that held his fate in the distance on his left. The skyscrapers shone regardless of whether the sun's beams tickled their faces, each car was new and well-washed, and every person walking the streets came from another world, dressed in everything from suits to exercise clothes, all more modern than anything he had seen outside of television. Torn between his desires to continue his timeless existence among the trees or dive headlong into a new world, Cortez chose to step forth and explore the second new landscape he had encountered that day. He made the same mistake he'd made on the other side of the park, stepping off the curb and into the street without checking for oncoming vehicles. A gleaming blue sports car, its engine soundless, stopped on a dime a fraction of second before colliding with him. This time, instead of honking in anger, the driver met Cortez's eyes and waved him on, encouraging him to continue. Cortez was about to retreat back into the safety of the trees when the other cars, following the blue car's lead, stopped and waited for him to cross. The Jews following Moses out of Egypt couldn't have been more surprised at the parting of the Red Sea.

The concrete underfoot in the new part of the city was cleaner than any Cortez had walked on before, with no caked gum, no stains, and no cracks. He looked back at the park and it shrank away. He turned into the city, following the urge to explore, but then turned again, walking parallel to the park so it would always be one block away from him. He passed a series of small shops that included a deli, a convenience store, and a dry cleaner's, all on the first floor of towering skyscrapers. He couldn't resist entering a coffee shop called Decant, a decision that led to the first and last time he fell in love.

He didn't see her at first; she was standing behind the counter making drink after drink for impatient customers. Instead, his eyes were drawn to the sparseness of the interior: the white walls lacking any decoration, and wide-open spaces between tables standing on concrete. He was enthralled by the level of absence the people in this part of the city could afford, because on his side of town everything was crammed into every available space in an attempt to validate the consumption of already scant resources. The customers demanded his inspection. Seen with his unfamiliar eyes, they were all unhurried, elegant, and methodical, as if the one place they should be on a workday's morning was the corner coffee shop. It wasn't until he had absorbed the swirling water that his eyes focused on the center of the vortex: Alara Chel. Her black hair was pulled back into the braid he would learn was her preference and covered in a branded hat, and the dimples on her cheeks flashed whenever her mouth moved. He let himself be pulled into the whirlpool of her presence, each footstep inspired by a higher power he assumed was the Lord himself. She smiled when she saw him.

"Line's over there," she said, tilting her head to the register on her right.

Cortez looked down at his feet. He was ashamed of being caught staring and knew he had been warned by the Bible about the class of thoughts now running through his head. He took a deep breath, then remembered his mother's admonition whenever she caught him retreating into himself. "Be polite." It had been her catchphrase as he was growing up.

"No, thank you," Cortez said.

Alara made no indication that Cortez's response was disjointed from her own statement. In fact, she used the opportunity to beckon him closer. She leaned over the counter. "It's your first time, isn't it?"

Cortez nodded, ashamed, thinking she was asking if it was the first time he had been struck by love's arrow.

"What do you want? It's on me."

The suggestion of a free drink caused Cortez's financial-sensitive brain to wrest control from his heart. "I don't know what you have," he said.

"Do you drink coffee?" she asked. Cortez knew he would never experience another sound as sweet as her voice if he lived to be a hundred and one. He shook his head no.

"I'll take care of you," she said, retreating back behind the espresso machine.

Cortez stepped back, ignorant of the annoyed looks from the rest of the customers. Among the regulars sitting down, the men in particular took issue with Cortez, all of them having tried speaking with her in the past, unable to get her to respond with anything beyond the demands of her job. Her one-word answers were aimed at ending conversations and hit their mark with legendary precision.

She handed out two drinks before catching Cortez's eye and handing him a frozen vanilla beverage with whipped cream. "Before you take this, you have to promise to come back," she said with a wink.

In that moment, Cortez would have promised to go to the far side of the world and retrieve the retreating moon. All she had to do was ask. He nodded, then tasted his drink. He had never before tasted anything as good as that drink, and never did again, because in each sip was the certainty that he had come in contact with one of God's angels. By the time the drink was finished, he was the world's newest sufferer of its oldest addiction: the high one received from obsessive love.

# CHAPTER SIX

THE TIDES of the coffee shop ebbed and flowed throughout the day amidst the all-encompassing smell of roasted, ground, and brewed coffee. At some points, when the tide was out, there was a mere trickle of customers, and the baristas would resume paused conversations. This ability, speaking on a different timescale than the one displayed by clocks, was the first thing new hires learned, and was the reason Alara never thought twice when Cortez responded with an odd statement after his momentary retreat into himself. When the tide was in, wave after wave of customers came crashing down, overflowing the space and spilling out onto the streets. The employees stood tall against the onslaught, immovable pillars until the end of their shift.

Cortez couldn't find the strength to leave Alara's orbit even after he finished his drink. He had no urge to escape from the public and head back to his part of the city, even as the day dragged on and the other customers questioned how someone could sit so long without doing any work. He snuck glances at Alara, taking great care not to stare, though the one thing he wanted was to inspect every aspect of her face free from social expectations to look away. As the sun began to set, Cortez realized he hadn't eaten. He took his bagged lunch from his backpack and ate in small, distracted bites. The banana, which he saved for last, had been compressed at some point in the day, leaving a third of it soft and mushy. During meals at the picnic table, he would toss the soft parts of the banana on the ground and watch the birds fly down from the overhead wires to inspect the rejected food. On the day he met Alara Chel, each bite of the fruit was cooked until soft by the heat coursing through his veins, so he didn't notice when part of it was softer than the rest. The burning questions in his heart threatened to turn his shirt into ashes. He wanted to know what foods she liked to eat, where she'd grown up, how many times a week she went out to eat. The most trivial details were, to him, the most pressing, because they were the ones nobody could find out without being allowed into her gravitational pull.

THERE WERE STILL a few hours left in the day when Alara said goodbye to her coworkers, took off her apron, and left her station behind. She emerged from behind the counter with parts of her apron visible over the top edge of her shoulder bag. The bag hung loose from her shoulders, a relaxed fabric that reminded Cortez of the hammock in the picture his mother kept on display of her homeland, Mexico. Alara wore all black: a tight-fitting polo and pants that highlighted the curves running from her hips to her thighs. Cortez, along with every other male in the space, noticed her robust femininity, though Cortez was the only one to drop his gaze before crossing the chasm into lust. Looking down at his shoes served a double purpose, because although he hadn't been able to think of anything but Alara since the moment he saw her, he also didn't want her to pay attention to him when there wasn't a counter protecting them from each other, and looking at his shoes ensured he wouldn't have to reciprocate her potential acknowledgment.

Alara knew Cortez had stayed in the coffee shop all day. She'd thought he was lost when she first saw him. They were both Hispanic and around the same age—facts that inspired a particular kinship with him. Her decision to give him a free drink had fulfilled the urge to help him find his way. The employees gave away free drinks all the time, so she didn't think twice about it. She thought it odd that the young man had combed his hair with obvious precision without having the clothes to match. In her experience, men who cared that much about their hair wore suits, drove expensive cars, and had an outsized view of their importance in the world. It was one of the perks of her job that she could ignore men like that when they tried to learn more about her; it was her purpose to put them in their place. She had kept tabs on Cortez out of the corner of her eye and knew he hadn't been working while in her dominion, instead sitting and watching the rest of the world around him as if he was born yesterday.

She held her head high while she walked out of Decant. An older lady sitting by the door, a regular who came in for a latte each afternoon before caring for her grandkids, commanded her attention by looking at her face as she approached. "Heading home?" she said.

Alara looked down at the lady and smiled. "All done for the day."

"Enjoy the sunshine."

"I plan on it."

It was the sort of clipped conversation Alara preferred. There was no divulging of information, no questioning of motives. She was the master of trite, memorized statements that were simple acknowledgments of existing in a shared space.

Behind her, Cortez packed his bag. He waited until she left

the coffee shop before standing up, telling himself he should be heading back to his side of the city. "Excuse me," he asked the young man still seated next to where he'd spent the bulk of his day. "What time is it?"

After the man glanced at his watch, he told Cortez it was minutes after four. Cortez didn't thank him for the information and left. Deciding he had seen enough of the city, he walked towards the park instead of going back the way he came. The trees in the distance promised both shade and security from the judging eyes of the people he passed. At the end of the block, he looked left and right for oncoming cars before he crossed the street and turned right. Ahead of him, on the park's edge, Alara was visible for an instant before she turned inside and was lost among the trees. Cortez's heart leapt into his throat as hurried after her. He had heard about the miracles Jesus performed but never in his life thought he would be on the receiving end of such a gift. Destiny was once more smiling down on him by placing her in his path. Mindful of appearances, he tried his best to walk at a relaxed pace when every fiber of his being urged him to run to where he last saw her. When he arrived at the spot where he saw her enter the park, he followed her into the shadows.

Alara frequented the park on the days she got out of work early enough to enjoy the sunshine. On days it was raining, she would sit in the library instead, reading until there was just enough light left in the day to avoid walking home in the shadows. She'd learned long ago not to go into the park during the night. The first and last time she stayed after the sun had gone down, she had emerged from the park and was waiting to cross the street when a car rolled to a stop and the male driver asked her how much for the night. He grew angry when she ignored him, putting on his hazards and stepping out of the vehicle. When she informed him she had no idea what he was talking about, the man asked her what she was doing at the edge of the park at night if not looking to be purchased by the hour. She ran until she got home and, collapsing through her front door, promised herself never to get caught in that situation again. The danger of the encounter didn't affect her as much as the man's belief that she was available for a price. Though it didn't last for more than a minute, and the potential customer now knew better, his momentary belief had wounded her delicate pride.

She walked to her favorite spot—a bench with its back to the trees that overlooked an open lawn—sat down, and began to read. Books had been her obsession for as long as she could remember. When she'd first learned to read, it was a way of signaling her independence. Now that she was older, it was her escape from the demands of the modern world. Her financial troubles were left behind, the questions about her purpose in life put on hold, and her insatiable curiosity about the experience of others were all remedied by ink on paper. She was reading *Love in the Time of Cholera*. Before work, she had read about Fermina Daza's rejection of Florentino Ariza, and it had haunted her mind while her body continued the familiar motions of her job. It was the saddest thing she had ever read and had created an atmosphere inside her soul where any act of witnessed injustice stirred tears she hid with stubbornness. If she had been one of the trees behind her, her leaves would have wilted, indifferent to the seasons of the year, instead under the spell of the seasons of her heart. On that park bench, alone with her book, Alara Chel existed in perpetual autumn.

Cortez hopped off the paved path when he spotted her in the distance. Between leaving the road and finding her he had walked without thinking, allowing his heart to lead his feet. He'd walked with the certainty he would find her, and he had taken a few turns that made no sense to his brain. His belief in destiny was justified when he found his nymph on a bench where the trees met an open lawn. He watched her from behind a tree. Walkers and joggers passed by without her lifting her eyes from the page. Children played in the open space ahead of her and she was deaf to their shouts. Cortez walked deeper into the woods, away from the path, careful not to step on any twigs, a sound that might betray his position. In truth, he could have yelled and Alara wouldn't have noticed. As he stood bewitched by the slow rise and fall of her shoulders with each breath she took, a group of young men came to the open area in front of her and began playing soccer. The leanest and most muscular of the group took off their shirts with glances in her direction without any reaction from her. While she read, she shared with Cortez an absolute focus on the task at hand—they were both lost to the rest of the world around them.

WITHOUT CONSULTING her watch or phone, Alara closed the book, put it into her backpack, and stood up. She looked at the sky, confirming her decision to leave by the position of the sun. The soccer ball rolled to a stop as every player watched her walk away. There were other, closer spaces where they could play, but none held so beautiful a prize. They came for her and she had no idea they existed. It was a curse many men who came across Alara Chel fell victim to, but none bothered to study her the way Cortez did. He was watching for ways he could fill a role in her life, an access point that would provide a way to prove his worth. His first role, however, was to make sure his heart didn't combust before he got the chance.

Cortez was torn when Alara walked back towards her side of the city. Questions about her emerged in his soul. He wondered what she was reading, if she always read in the park, and what type of men she liked if not the athletes on display. More pressing, he wanted to know where she was going. It was also past the time he should be home. His mother would be waiting for him if she had managed to pull herself from her depressive episode, though her low points never lasted for just one day. Never having been consumed by love before, and therefore never learning how to navigate the situation, he gave into his curiosity and followed Alara back to her side of the city. In his mind, destiny had put her in his path, and it was his role to follow through. Her beauty did make him wonder about his true intentions, and in an effort to assuage his guilty conscience he convinced himself he would try to convince her to come to church.

Yes, his role was to save her soul. The best way to do so was to learn more about her, including where she lived, and to protect her, making sure she lived long enough to hear the word of God next to him on Sundays.

There was a half-block minimum between them at all times. He had never followed someone before but had seen enough movies for a rough idea of how it should be done. Ducking into entrances, stopping to window shop while keeping the target in the corner of his eye. It wasn't difficult to follow her because she never thought she was worth following, so she took the simplest path home. Alara's path went straight into a part of the city Cortez had never seen before, past buildings that reached for the sky with unnatural determination. Cortez's anxiety increased at the same rate as his distance from the park, and by the time Alara left the skyscrapers behind and turned into a residential area with tree-lined roads, Cortez had taken a white pill to combat the certainty he had gone too far from home, a sailor on concrete seas who had lost sight of land for the first time.

The streetlights flickered on as the lack of light from the setting sun triggered their sensors. Cortez gave himself two more blocks before he would turn around. He was questioning whether he remembered the way back. He stayed farther away from her now, more than a block behind, taking greater care to stay hidden now that there were fewer options for him to utilize for cover on his stealthy mission. It was an unnecessary precaution; she never looked behind her. Cortez was about to turn around, planning on returning to Decant the next day to see her again, when she turned off the road, too soon to be another intersection. Cortez quickened his pace, closed the distance, then slowed before coming to where Alara had turned. She had crossed a concrete courtyard with a series of weed-filled planters. More weeds were poking up through the cracks between concrete slabs. Cortez was comforted by the overgrowth. Its presence meant that the people living on this side of the city still had to deal with life seeping through the cracks of their pristine exteriors. The buildings around the courtyard were made of brick, and all of them stood three stories high. Movement flashed from across the space. It was Alara, climbing the exposed stairs that ran between units. Cortez exhaled, grateful he hadn't stormed into the space in pursuit. If he had, she would be staring down at him right then, and there was no way to explain why the man who had received a free drink earlier in the day was standing outside her home.

Cortez saw her turn into a unit on her left on the third floor. Some of the units had windows facing the courtyard, but the one she entered was on a corner between the far building and the one on his right. There would be no window where she could see him approach, but that also meant there was no window where he could see what she was like alone. Even if he crossed the courtyard and took the steps she had just climbed—which he had no intention of doing—there was nothing for him there but a door. He kept walking past the courtyard and turned, walking along the back side of the building on the courtyard's right. He could see inside the units on the ground floor through vertical blinds. Some were occupied by families, some by lone individuals, but each space gave off the particular blue light indicative of turned-on televisions. Cortez saw some shows he recognized, and one person was watching the news. He stopped beneath where he believed Alara's unit was located. There was a dull yellow light, instead of the typical blue, on in one of the third-floor units. The rest on that level were dark or had the blinds shut. Cortez stood beneath the tree that stood outside the lit window and took stock of its ability to support his weight. Deciding it could support him, he began to climb.

Cortez had never been with a woman. He was old enough to understand that the body had its own needs, but without ever experiencing them himself, he had never learned to think about how his own actions might be interpreted as driven by sexual desire. He climbed with an innocence born out of his sheltered existence, out of mere curiosity, because he did in fact just want to see how Alara lived when she was alone. He got high enough to see the ceiling above the kitchen when the loud clearing of a throat drew his attention from below.

"And just what do you think you're doing, young man?" a middle-aged woman with short hair, taking her dog for a walk, said to him with one hand on her hip. The dog continued walking, following its nose, and turned around when it reached the end of the leash, staring at its human for the rude interruption.

Cortez had been yelled at before by his mother, and various other women in school or church when he was a child, but each one had been either Hispanic or Black and never used the language he associated with old sitcom reruns. He almost laughed at the perfect replica the woman was able to produce, and he was certain that if he opened his mouth the chuckle would escape his lips. Instead, all he did was stare.

"Well?"

Cortez began climbing down. When he got back to ground

level, he discovered the woman came up to his armpit. He ran away before she could utter another word and didn't stop until he had crossed the park once more and climbed the seven flights of steps to his own home.

From inside her dark apartment, Alara witnessed a young man with a backpack running away from a lady walking her dog. She had just gotten out of the bathroom and was at the window to close the blinds—which she always did before turning on the light—when the rapid movement down on the street in front of her neighbor's unit drew her attention. She never imagined that the man fleeing was there because of her. A call to the police would have been Alara's next step if the lady, whom Alara had assumed had been robbed, hadn't continued walking while shaking her head with disappointment. Alara closed the blinds, warmed up leftovers from the day before, and dove headfirst into the pages of her book once more.

# CHAPTER SEVEN

WEDNESDAYS MEANT CHURCH. Their faith's midweek refresh. Cortez didn't look forward to it, and he didn't dread it; rather, it was just another part of the routine, a task to be completed. He had gone to Decant earlier in the day, looking for Alara. It must have been her day off, or she was working at a different time, because she wasn't there. He didn't know which drink to order, and when he sat down to wait for her empty-handed, one of the baristas told him to get out by informing him that tables were for paying customers only. She had been terrified of breaking the news to Cortez and apologized with a shaky voice. Cortez left without a word, followed by the stares of the customers in the shop, and spent the rest of the afternoon sitting on Alara's park bench, imagining which of the smells that reached his nose lingered from her presence in the same spot the night before.

The question of whether they would attend the Wednesday night service at all plagued Cortez during his walk home at the same time he used to get off work at the factory. His mother's depression had showed no signs of abating. She had been missing from his life since Sunday, and when he left that morning she was still trapped in her room, not going to work.

Cortez never questioned why her job didn't fire her. Thinking about job loss forced Cortez to recall his own, this time accompanied by a sickening possibility: his mother had found out about the events at work without him telling her. A sense of shame welled up inside him, one that caused him to use a tree for support and retch, though nothing came out. The knowledge that his mother would confront him if she did know, wanting to hear his side of the story, comforted him, and he was able to continue home after taking a white pill. The story of the Virgin Mary popped into his head while he walked, and he came to believe that her depression had been caused by him without her ever having learned the information. The immaculate conception of his mother's depression.

His mother had managed to pull herself from the bedroom's darkness and was in the kitchen frying plantains when Cortez arrived. She was wearing her light blue dress and had foregone the head covering, saving it for Sunday. "Hello, my son," she said when Cortez walked in. "How was your day?"

"It was good," Cortez said. Whenever anyone asked, his day was good, no matter how it had been in reality. Nobody ever asked him to elaborate. Even though that day hadn't been good —he knew that for the rest of his life a day without seeing Alara could never be good—the phrase prevented him from having to talk about it with his mother, and she kept moving forward like a train after it had left the station.

"Mine too. After you left, I got out of bed and went into work. They were mad, but they'll get over it," she said with a laugh. Cortez wondered what it would be like to be untouchable at a job.

She sat the spatula down on the edge of the frying pan and looked at Cortez as if seeing her son for the first time. The gaze made him uncomfortable. "You know you're my inspiration, don't you? Waking up and going to work each day, without interruption." Cortez looked at her mouth while she spoke, not wanting to look in her eyes. Understanding she was making her son uncomfortable, she picked up the spatula and poked at the frying fruit. "You remind me so much of your father."

"You've told me," he replied.

Bringing up his father was the worst part of his mother's depressive episodes. She did it every time she emerged. The man had abandoned them when Cortez was born. His mother was convinced that if she and Cortez were able to make it on their own, to demonstrate their worth, he would come back and they could be together again. Cortez did all he could to help with her mission, but it had been over twenty years and there had been no sign of him, not even a postcard. As a boy, Cortez had hoped he could impress his absent father through school. It hadn't taken long to realize it wasn't going to happen. Then, with his first job delivering newspapers, he wondered what financial empires he would create to entice his father's return, but those dreams had been dashed when he became over-whelmed and had to rely on his mother's help to get the work done in the early morning hours. That was how he had come to believe the one avenue available was the Church, though now that he had met Alara Chel, he wondered if a quality woman by his side would be enough to impress the man he'd never known.

"Get a plate," Cortez's mother told him. Cortez retrieved one from the cabinet and stood next to his mother while she put the plantains from the frying pan onto it, creating a stack that multiplied with each scoop. Jesus feeding thousands with a few loaves of bread. She grabbed another plate, put some food onto it for herself that didn't make a dent in Cortez's pile, then commanded him to eat.

. . .

THE PAIR CLEANED the kitchen and left for church when their meager meal was finished. His mother talked the entire walk, releasing every word she had saved up during her two days in darkness. She talked about the gossip at the hotel, she talked about the things she wanted to do the following weekend, and she discussed the storylines of her favorite shows like they were old friends she hadn't seen in a while. Cortez pretended to listen the whole time, interjecting various expressions he knew would make her believe he cared what she was saying. Out of nowhere, she turned to him and declared that she hadn't heard anything about him recently. "How's Simeon doing?" she asked.

"He's been good. Sitting a lot," Cortez said. He smiled at his joke, the same one Simeon had made about himself.

His mother hit him in the arm with the back of her hand. It wiped the smile off his face. "What's the matter with you? Making fun of that poor boy's condition is mean! He's had a hard life."

Cortez looked down at the sidewalk. "I know."

They walked the rest of the way to church without saying another word.

His mother blossomed as soon as they entered the school building where service was held. Cortez stood by her side while she pretended her life was worthy of envy, as if she hadn't spent the intervening days between her last appearance and this one in a cocoon of blankets. The service was led by an older member, one of the church's first. He was on the church council and stood in front of the few dozen members of the congregation wearing a suit that looked like it had been worn all day and for many years beforehand. When he began, he informed the congregation that their priest had become their former priest, having left on a mission trip to Mexico. Cortez's mother beamed with pride at the information. She was from Mexico, had been born there before coming to their current city, and Cortez had heard about his ancestor's position in the Church for as long as he could remember. The way she said it, he was born to lead people to Christ: it was in his blood.

"And so, I'll be leading us for the time being," the new leader said. Wednesday services were less formal than Sundays, and they spoke about real-life experiences instead of dissecting the Bible. The suited man was notorious for wiping his nose with a light purple handkerchief he kept in his right pants pocket, and he did so multiple times while he spoke about giving to the poor. Soon after he began his story, Cortez stopped listening, instead focusing on how many times the man withdrew his handkerchief and wondering why he was talking about his own charity when it was supposed to be between the giver and God. The entire talk took less than half an hour, far short of the typical length, and Cortez was grateful when they were told to go out and spread the word.

The real reason the Wednesday service was held was so that the congregation would have a reason to gather before going back out onto the streets in search of more parishioners. Whoever had begun the practice, which had been in place since before the previous priest had arrived, didn't trust the people to go out on their own without worship beforehand. There were few reunions after the short service, since most had taken place when people first arrived. It was still a work night, after all, and everyone wanted to finish their holy task with time to relax at home before bed. Cortez's mother led the way to her chosen spot for the night's work, a Mexican restaurant they went to twice a year, on each of their birthdays.

"We'll be the ones to save the Church," she said with certainty when they arrived.

. . .

THE RESTAURANT HAD BEEN in the city for as long as anyone could remember. Its owners had claimed to be the first Mexicans to arrive, and legend had it they'd created the restaurant so the arriving diaspora would have somewhere to congregate. The food was nothing spectacular, but the atmosphere had created a Mexican religion whose adherents chose their country as their deity of choice. Cortez and his mother took up position outside, determined to talk to the people waiting for one of the coveted tables. With a wait that could go over an hour each night, there was plenty of time for them to discuss the power of God's grace.

The air was heavy with the smell of frying meats, fresh tortillas, and perfume. The plantain in Cortez's belly had been delicious but was no match for the smells emanating from countless Mexican dishes. When his stomach rumbled, he reminded himself that some things were more important than meals. In particular, the sustenance his soul would receive if they were successful in bringing new people to Christ.

Mexican music could be heard from outside. Cortez, who had learned Spanish from his mother but never spoke it, listened to his mother talk in her native language with the people waiting to eat dinner. At first, the people assumed she was waiting for a table as well. They would chat about where in the country they came from, if they knew this or that person, and when they'd first arrived in the city. Once they were deep in conversation, she would switch and begin talking about the Church, extolling the virtues of her particular place of worship, and would share how instrumental faith had been in her successful transition into the English-speaking city. Most of the people listened until their table was called, but some adopted looks of disgust when they realized her ploy. There were people who belonged to other churches who would want to discuss matters of faith with her, but when she realized they already belonged to a church, Cortez's mother would find a way out of the conversation.

Diners began avoiding the lingering pair when they realized the woman and her son weren't waiting for a table until a man and woman, both old enough to be retired, sat down and took more interest in Cortez than in anything his mother was saying. It started when they asked if he was Mexican as well, after hearing his mother came from a city in the Yucatán Peninsula.

"Well, he's my son," Cortez's mother said as an explanation.

"Full Mexican?" the older woman clarified, in English. She had white hair and the air of a patient librarian. Her husband was bald and thin everywhere except his belly.

"Full Mexican," Cortez said.

"Where's your father from?" the woman asked.

"Mexico City," Cortez answered. His mother shifted in her seat. She had a habit of shutting down whenever Cortez's father was brought up, but her earlier emergence from her room and subsequent comparison of Cortez to his father had prepared her for the interaction. She was silent, but present, and paid attention.

"We're from Mexico City," the man growled. He wasn't mean, just serious from a life of scraping by to support his family while struggling to master a foreign language.

"What was his name?" the wife asked.

Cortez looked at his mother. She never spoke his name, not wanting to invoke the associated pain the man had caused by his exit. It was as if his name had the power to break her attachment to Cortez and suck the strength she received from her son's continued existence. "It's not important," Cortez said.

"Well, what if we know him?" the man said, defending his wife's question.

"Even if you do, we don't," Cortez said. He was a moment away from ignoring them when he remembered why he and his mother were outside the popular restaurant in the first place: to find more people to worship alongside them at church. It was this duty that gave him strength, even though he wanted the conversation to be over. In a flash, he imagined the old couple had children, each old enough to have their own families. They might have friends, or siblings, who would all have descendants of their own. Sitting next to him, asking him questions he'd rather not answer, they could be the big fish he had been hunting, the prize that would elevate him in the Church, bring back his father, and end his mother's torment whenever the man was discussed.

"My father is the Lord," he said, inspired. In that moment he became his mother's angel, emerging from heaven to save her from the pain of rejection.

The wife and husband looked at each other. "So you're Jesus, and this must be Mary," the man said.

Cortez's mother's jaw went limp, her mouth open. "His name was Diego . . . Albalate," she said when she pulled herself together.

"We knew a Diego Albalete," the white-haired wife said. She had the devil's wicked smile. "He came here about twenty years ago."

"Doubt it's the same one," Cortez's mother said, exhausted.

The wife turned her attention to Cortez. "You kind of look like him," she continued, turning the knife. She looked at her husband. "What ever became of him?"

"After he dated Rosalín? I'm not sure."

"Rosalín was our daughter's best friend," the wife explained to Cortez and his mother. "Beautiful girl."

Cortez didn't expect the anger on his mother's face. He knew he had to take action, to save his mother from the past and, with any luck, convince these two they were the seeds in the soil that would produce fruit in the church's orchard.

"Do you pray?" Cortez asked, trying to change the subject.

"What's it to you?" the husband answered.

"Our church meets on Sunday. There's always room for two more."

The couple laughed. Just then, they were informed their table was ready. Cortez's mother spat on the ground when they got up and walked away with the small steps typical for people at their advanced age. "They'd better pray the Lord doesn't strike them down for their wickedness," she said. Cortez held out hope they would show up on Sunday, even though they'd never inquired about the location, not knowing the couple would be dead before the start of the following Sunday's service.

The hostess studied Cortez and his mother, then frowned. Within minutes, the restaurant's owner was outside telling them to leave.

"I can't have you sitting out here scaring the customers!" he bellowed.

Cortez looked past the rage and saw another opportunity. The owner of the most popular restaurant in town would be a wonderful addition to their congregation. Maybe, if they were lucky, he would provide the food for their after-service meal. "Our church meets every Sunday at nine," he said. "Would you like the address?" He used his sweetest voice, one he reserved for asking favors from his mother.

"No, I don't want the address!" the man yelled. He looked at Cortez's mother. "What the hell is the matter with him?" he asked.

"He's trying to save your soul, that's what's the matter with him! He's out here, among you sinners, trying to save you. One day, all of you will be sorry when you realize you dismissed a great man!" With that, she grabbed her son, and together they walked away.

Cortez waited until the music from the restaurant had faded into the distance. "Do you really think I'm a great man?" Cortez asked.

"Not yet, but you will be," his mother said. All the hope she had in the world rested on him, and she lived off the sustenance its sweet nectar provided.

# CHAPTER EIGHT

CORTEZ TOLD his mother he was leaving and let her assume he was headed to the ice cream factory. The morning was overcast, creating a shadow over the city that confused the night creatures and convinced them to stay in the streets until well after their daytime neighbors had emerged. In addition to passing men selling contraband and women selling sex, Cortez walked by two traffic accidents caused by the increased number of people out of their homes, neither serious, which clogged traffic in both directions and caused stranded drivers to lean out of their windows shouting at the unfortunate souls who'd suffered through the collision. Police were present at both scenes. Cortez kept his eyes trained straight ahead, in case any of those he passed had been present at the drug deal that cost him his job.

The park was a welcome relief from the congestion. Inside its borders, there was plenty of space for all who chose to enter. Since it was still cool, few people had the desire to enjoy the open space. Some of those present were the ones who had been out the night before, stranded in the daylight. There were home-less people on benches and groups of young men looking for trouble; in more than one gathering, Cortez saw a replay of the drug deal he had experienced because of Simeon's greed. Humans weren't the only confused animals. Bats screeched as they shot through the air, opossums walked about on their two hind legs, raccoons looted garbage cans, and deer gathered together in the park's open spaces. The park, on that overcast morning, stood at the intersections of nature and civilization, night and day.

Cortez walked on a ray of light, above the detritus, inspired by the certainty Alara would be working that day. His night had been sleepless, filled with tossing, turning, and thinking, stuck in the space between full wakefulness and dreams. Thoughts of Alara had filled his head, and he feared the day in their future when he would be recognized by her neighbor after being invited to her home. She was still in his head on the rare instances he managed to dream. All he could remember from them was her smell. He couldn't place it, but he knew that he enjoyed it, was addicted to it. It was nature, sweetness, and pride, all rolled into one, and if he could find the scent he'd find a way to surround himself with it wherever he went. When he'd woken up, he'd known that the day would bring him into contact with her, with a certainty born from never having his heart broken before.

Nothing bothered him as he crossed the park. Both animals and people recognized he was a man on a mission bestowed upon him by a power they couldn't understand or experience. Older individuals out for their morning walk, awoken by various body processes each morning and never getting enough sleep, held a faint sense of recognition when they saw the way he walked, but it had been so long since they had witnessed a young man in the grips of love that they forgot his affliction and assumed he was suffering from chronic narcissism.

The clouds' shadows ended at the edge of the park. Cortez attributed their disappearance to the power of Alara Chel, certain in the knowledge that her radiance was even bright enough to chase away a storm. Controlling the weather was just one more attribute she possessed—he knew her power had no limits. If he ever managed to convince her to join him in worship, to save her soul, he knew she would be the one to save his church, the spark that would ignite the flame and light up the world. A moment of panic set in when he imagined the world discovering her magic for the first time. He had no doubt they would be as enamored with her as him. For her sake, he should keep her to himself, to keep her safe.

He laughed, knowing that saving her and, as a result of her conversion, helping save the Church was what he had been put on the earth to accomplish. Still, the darkness of stifling her had entered his heart as he crossed into her side of the city, and he would struggle to keep it contained until he took his last breath.

HAVING LEARNED his lesson the day before about needing to purchase a drink in order to sit inside the coffee shop, Cortez had taken a few dollars from the money he shared with his mother. She trusted him, never having a reason to doubt his good sense, and left it uncounted in a jar high up in the cabinet next to their refrigerator. Financial matters gave her a headache, and going to the bank made her constipated, so she reserved these tasks to one day a month, when she would have a plan in place to suffer in peace.

Decant was filled with people when he walked in. The line was to the door, and every seat was filled. Alara wasn't behind the counter. Cortez took his place at the back of the line behind a bicyclist who still wore his helmet and specialty shoes, which made a metallic snap with each step he took. A young woman wearing a dark gray skirt and matching sport coat stood behind him a moment later. She talked on the phone the entire time, her conversation filled with legal jargon as she told her assistant what needed to be done. The line creeped along at the same pace the drinks were handed off to customers who had already paid. It was a delicate balancing act, one the employees working the register had experience navigating, knowing they shouldn't try to move faster because on days they themselves made drinks they expected to be shown the same courtesy.

The young man at the register had long hair tied in a ponytail. It was obvious he was young from the red blemishes on his skin. When Cortez got to the front of the line, the young man asked what he wanted.

"What's the cheapest thing you have?" Cortez asked. The menu hanging overhead had numerous offerings, with names Cortez had never seen before, each priced higher than he had expected. His hand was in his pocket, gripping the cash with a sweaty palm.

"Um." The young man turned around, looked at the menu, and pointed to a section of small font in the lower right-hand corner. "A small coffee."

"I'll take one of those." He counted out the dollars and handed them over. Beneath their hands was an overflowing tip jar. While the young man working the register counted out the transaction's change, Cortez's mind contracted when he thought about the concept of leaving a tip himself. He didn't want to stand out from the other customers, and judging from the amount already in the jar, he guessed every previous customer had placed their change inside. In reality, the Decant employees, knowing the power of peer pressure, placed money from the cash register in the tip jar before the start of the shift. So, when Cortez received the coins that constituted his change, he placed them inside the tip jar before moving to the exact spot Alara had handed him the drink, hoping that his presence at the location of their previous encounter would somehow make her appear on the other side of the counter.

"I have your coffee right here," the young man called out to Cortez. Cortez went back to the register and accepted the drink.

The coffee Cortez had sampled before now was better classified as brown water. It was served at church and left sitting for hours. On the rare occasions Cortez had a cup, he added two sugars and enough milk to change the drink's color to a light brown. Decant's coffee didn't change color at all with the equivalent amount of milk, but he tasted it anyway, finding it much too bitter even with two sugars inside. He poured some out, then added more milk before tasting again and still finding it not to his liking. The process was repeated three more times, and in the end half the original coffee was in the trash, replaced with the same amount of milk. Content with his concoction, Cortez put the lid back on and scanned the room for somewhere to wait for his beloved.

She must have entered when he was busy adding milk. Alara sat in one of the two corner chairs, leaning over and engaged in conversation with a clean-cut young man. Cortez's heart entered his throat when he realized he, along with the rest of the people in the room, didn't exist for the couple. Her conversation partner was handsome, with a square jaw and long eyelashes, and tan skin that was the result of mixed parentage. His clothes were cut just for him, the shirt highlighting the size of his arms and leaving space for the vein on his biceps, and his pants ended right above his ankle.

The couple never noticed his stare. Cortez watched them for a full five minutes, not blinking, not moving a muscle, torn between jealousy and an appreciation that she hadn't been a figment of his imagination. She was real, was in the same room as him, breathing the same air, and that knowledge gave him the strength to stand tall against the torrential storm of hatred he held for the man next to her. His stupor lasted until they stood up. He scanned the room, found an open seat with a table, and sat down in time to watch them walk, together, to the open spot in the counter Alara would pass through to begin her workday. She was wearing the same outfit as the last time Cortez had seen her, with the same shoulder bag, but this time her black hair hung down below her shoulder blades. It was the most beautiful hair in the world, and he was struck by the sudden urge to hide inside her locks and watch her exist, the same way he'd hidden in the trees when he watched her in the park.

BEFORE SHE WENT TO WORK, Alara gave her companion a hug and a kiss. She didn't see the person doubled over, a sharp pain gripping his stomach, at one of the tables. Her boyfriend, Remy Moncard, walked her to work a few times each week. Every time he did, he made sure they were there early, so they could sit down and talk for a while before she had to clock in. What she thought was a sweet gesture was, in truth, a way for Remy to display his trophy to the men he knew watched her at the coffee shop. Before Remy left, she offered him a drink, but he refused, the same way he always did. Alara enjoyed their dance routine, performed in front of everyone in the room, lost in their own world for the few moments before she had to face the day's customers. Remy enjoyed the performance.

After Remy left, Alara twisted her hair into the braid Cortez came to associate with her, put on her hat and apron, and got to work. From the table against the wall, Cortez watched her move with a dancer's grace as she made drink after drink. His coffee had become cold by the time the pain in his stomach subsided, and he drank with each large gulp spaced out, making the drink last as long as possible—it wasn't hard, because coffee wasn't high on his list of preferred beverages. When the line died down to a trickle, and the employees were able to catch their breath, Cortez got the urge to approach her. There was a long internal struggle—and a white pill swallowed—before he worked up the nerve to stand up, and the war continued with each step on his approach to the counter.

He stood opposite Alara, waiting for her to acknowledge his presence. When she didn't, he worked up the courage to say the first word by reminding himself the Church depended on his action. "Hello," he whispered.

She didn't hear him.

The first barrier of speech was the hardest to cross; after that, the words trickled out. "Hello," he said, loud enough to be certain she heard. She looked up at him from over the machine she stood in front of and all air left Cortez's lungs. He longed for his inhaler, still in his backpack where he was sitting.

"Hi," she said. She didn't recognize the pale, timid-looking man standing before her.

"I came back," Cortez said. The advice of the Church, to smile when greeting new people, reverberated through his skull, and he forced his lips to display his teeth.

"Good for you," Alara said, smiling back at him. Their smiles, though the same classification of gesture, were leagues apart in quality. Similar to the way a chihuahua and a great dane are both dogs, but on different ends of the size spectrum. Cortez's smile displayed small teeth and bright red gums, and nervous lines formed where his lips met his cheeks. Alara's smile, on the other hand, showed perfect, straight, bright white teeth, and was so well practiced from years of charming customers that she was able to flash it without a second thought.

When Alara went back to her task behind the machine, Cortez tried to think of something to say that would keep her attention. His mother had spent years drilling into his head the etiquette when introducing oneself, and he blurted out, "My name is Cortez," in a sudden flash of inspiration.

Alara looked up at the miserable creature. He looked lost and inspired her pity. Something about him reminded her that she had given that same individual a drink two days before. "I made you promise to come back," she murmured, more as a reminder to herself than an attempt to continue their communication. It wasn't the first time a man had believed she wanted to see him again, but he was the most pitiful individual who had followed through.

"And I did," Cortez said. A dog expecting a treat for performing a mastered trick.

Alara chuckled. "My name's Alara."

No man had ever been as inspired by a single word as Cortez was when he first heard her name, standing in a coffee shop in a part of the city where he didn't belong. It was a breath of fresh air, filling his lungs with vitality, and in that moment he realized she was more effective than any prescribed inhaler.

"Did you already get a drink? The first one was free, the rest you have to pay for," Alara informed him.

"I did." Cortez pointed to the empty cup on the table. His backpack was on the ground next to the chair.

Alara abandoned her task and leaned with a hand on the counter. She enjoyed getting him out of his shell. "What did you get?" Alara said.

"A coffee. I already finished it though."

"Well, you know refills are free."

Cortez lit up. "Free" had been his favorite word, before he discovered Alara's name.

Alara could read the young man like a book and enjoyed his delight. She leaned farther forward, as if divulging a secret. "Just take your cup to the register and tell them you want a refill."

Though Cortez still held a library of words in his heart, he knew their interaction had drawn to a close. He retrieved his cup, got his refill, and spent the rest of the afternoon content with being in Alara's presence. Knowing nobody could ask him to leave, since he was a customer, was the best part.

# CHAPTER NINE

REMY MONCARD CAME BACK around the time Cortez started thinking about going home. Cortez's stomach dropped to his feet, and it lingered there until he curled his toes within his shoes to force it back up. Remy had changed into a suit and walked in carrying a bouquet. Everyone stared as he walked up to the counter on the opposite side of Alara, the spot Cortez had stood, and informed her they were going out to dinner for their anniversary. The other employees smiled to themselves, delighted at having a new topic of conversation that would last for days. If there's one thing a group of young people in close proximity will do, it's gossip.

Alara told Remy she had planned on going to read in the park. "I didn't even remember it was our anniversary!" she said. Finding out Alara was in a relationship didn't dampen Cortez's resolve; in fact, he thought of the man as another thing she needed saving from.

"You go there after work every day," Remy said, rolling his eyes. Cortez took note of the information. "One whole year," Remy continued, saying it loud enough for everyone, including Cortez, to hear.

Alara's short shift ended minutes after Remy arrived, and soon Cortez watched the two of them leaving, Alara no longer wearing her job's required accessories. She complained about not having anything to wear.

"I look terrible next to you!" she said.

"Like you belong on the other side of the park," Remy said with a laugh. "Don't worry, we're going to buy you a new dress. It's part of the date."

Alara laughed, and heat crawled up Cortez's neck. He wanted to be the reason she laughed, and he wanted her with him in a new dress when they walked into church together. His bed called out to him from across the city, beckoning him home to the embrace of escape. It was the same call his mother succumbed to that began her disappearances, one he was able to ignore. His melancholy at seeing Alara leave with Remy was overpowered by wanting to continue existing in her presence, and for the second time that week he found himself following her after she got off work.

The pair went to a multilevel department store. Its exterior was white marble, one part of a larger building, and the name was written in indecipherable cursive. Cortez managed to stay hidden from their view while following them up one level. He hid in the men's shoe section while Alara tried on a dress and matching shoes. Another man, balding and wearing thick glasses, slid next to Cortez while he watched.

"She's gorgeous, isn't she?"

Cortez hadn't noticed the man approach. He was startled, his heart beating loud in his ears. "What are you talking about?" he said.

"You know. Did you think you're the only one who notices her?" The man showed Cortez his employee identification card. "They come in here every so often. Do you see the man helping them? It was his turn to take care of her."

The salesman next to Remy turned to Cortez and the balding individual and flashed a quick smile before returning to the customers. "I'll get the next time they come in," he said with a lizard-like lick of his lips.

Cortez shook his head. "I'm going to save her," he said, resolute.

"You'll need saving from her boyfriend if he ever catches you," he warned Cortez before leaving his side.

Remy paid for the change of clothes with a swipe of his card. Alara wore low black heels and a simple black dress that left little to the imagination. A bag provided by the store held her work clothes and shoes. Cortez saw Alara shake her head when Remy pointed to the makeup section of the store. He grew angry with her companion, not just for being the man by Alara's side, but for suggesting her face required compounds to enhance her beauty. The celebrating couple left the store without noticing the six eyes watching them, two from behind a rack of shoes.

Their actual date was at a restaurant next to the largest fountain Cortez had ever seen. He watched from outside the entrance as they were led to a table right next to the water. After hurrying to the opposite side of the fountain and taking his post on a stone bench with a good view of their table, he watched for the next hour while they enjoyed their meal. Cortez hadn't eaten since lunch but confused the hunger for the longing in his heart. Worrying about his mother never crossed his mind, and at that exact instant she was wondering where her son could be, fearing the worst, with a frozen pizza cooked and sliced for when he arrived.

"She's a beauty, isn't she?" an old man said. He was seated next to Cortez on the bench.

Cortez, sure this was another man who had fallen for

Alara's beauty, said that she was the most beautiful woman he had ever seen.

"The fountain, boy, I mean the fountain. The way the light sparkles around the edges of the water droplets before they come crashing down to earth. It's mesmerizing."

It sounded to Cortez like the man was describing an angel. His angel, Alara. They sat facing the fountain together, the old man watching the water and Cortez watching the couple, until Alara and Remy finished their meal. Their check paid for, they set off in the direction of Alara's house. Cortez followed from a distance, pleased with how well he tracked them without being seen.

They stood outside Alara's apartment for a few minutes, saying goodbye. Remy was asking to be let in, expecting to spend the night, but Alara told him she had work in the morning and didn't want to share her bed. She promised him she would come over tomorrow. Remy, not used to anyone telling him no, pushed back, but Alara was firm.

"I'm going to sleep as soon as I get upstairs," she said. The truth was, she had stopped reading her book at a pivotal moment, and she'd spent the majority of their date looking forward to what happened next. She had waited long enough, and she knew that if Remy came upstairs she wouldn't have a moment's peace. Most nights, she appreciated the company, but when she wanted to be alone there wasn't anything that could convince her otherwise. One of her fears was how she would handle moving in together, if it ever got to that point, but the scenario was far enough away that she didn't bother herself considering how she would navigate the situation.

Once Remy realized how pointless it was to push back against Alara's obstinacy, he kissed her, gave her a hug, and told her he'd see her tomorrow. He watched her walk up the stairs from inside the concrete courtyard before turning to leave.

Cortez ran down the block and turned onto the next street when he saw Remy turn around. There was no good reason for him to be in the area. He panicked when he realized he didn't know which way Remy would walk, knowing that Alara's companion might catch him lingering at the corner. He peeked around the corner and saw Remy walking right towards him. Cortez was lucky Remy was too lost in thought to notice the pair of eyes cutting through the darkness. Cortez started walking away from the corner, hoping that even if Remy was going in the same direction he'd never recognize the back of his head or his backpack. He turned around at the end of the block and saw Remy walking in the opposite direction. He was headed back towards the coffee shop and the high-rises. Cortez turned around, hurried forward, and followed Remy until he disappeared into a luxury apartment building.

LIFE in the city after the sun went down reminded Cortez of life he had seen in movies. He hadn't noticed while he was following the couple, but now he couldn't notice anything else. There were well-dressed people in restaurants, walking back from or going to late dinners, and shiny cars reflected the headlights of their fellow vehicles. Cortez took the scene in from outside Remy's apartment building and didn't see when his quarry reappeared at the entrance, letting in another woman.

Remy recognized Cortez from the coffee shop and was shocked to find him outside his building. They were about the same age, but a lifetime on different sides of the city had left them with little else in common. After he let the woman inside the building, he told her to wait inside the entrance. "There's something I have to take care of," he said. "I'll only be a minute." He left the building and approached Cortez, unnoticed.

"Have you been following me?" he said while standing next to Cortez, staring at the city alongside him.

Cortez had never been so terrified in his life. He had been yelled at before, and was scared each time it happened, but something in the coldness of Alara's friend's voice made his hair stand on end. It was all he could do to shake his head.

"Then why are you here?" Remy asked, without looking at Cortez, after seeing the denial out of the corner of his eye.

"I was in the area," Cortez responded.

Remy turned to face Cortez. He grabbed him by the front of his shirt. "Look, I don't know what kind of weird thing you have with Alara, but she's taken," he said. "Don't let me see you around here again." With that, Remy turned and started walking back into his building; Cortez downed a blue pill.

Seeing Alara on a date reminded Cortez of his own inexperience with spending intimate time with a woman. Once he'd recovered from Remy's threat, reminding himself that Alara's friend couldn't keep him from the coffee shop, he spent the rest of the walk home lost in thoughts of how he could keep a conversation going if he was alone with her. His first mistake was assuming the entire responsibility rested on his shoulders. As he walked back through the park, he scanned his memory for questions he had been asked when first meeting people, knowing he could never ask the specific questions about her peculiarities he wanted answered. Though he remembered meeting people at the factory, at church, and at school, he couldn't come up with a single piece of useful information. The nighttime people in the park didn't dare approach the young man who was muttering to himself; they thought he had been let loose by some benevolent caretaker, allowed to roam the paths at night because he couldn't be allowed out during the day for fear he'd scare anyone who saw him conversing with his own shadow. Cortez thought about the various television shows and movies he relied on for cues about proper social interaction. He remembered the characters dressed in their Sunday best, how they put their napkins on their laps to signal their politeness and smiled while looking their companions in the eye. For the life of him, he couldn't remember what they said.

His second mistake was assuming any strategy he came up with would even be effective in the heat of battle.

HIS MOTHER WAS WAITING for him when he got home. She was in her recliner, watching a telenovela, and Cortez knew right away from the angle of her chair that she was still wide awake. Still hoping for a miracle, he closed the door without making a sound.

The truth was that his mother had spent the entire night staring at the television without registering what was happening on-screen. Her son, the lone bright spot in her gloomy world, hadn't come home at his usual time. She knew he didn't make friends, and didn't have hobbies, so his disappearance was a mystery she couldn't ignore. In hopes his nose might lead him back, she had made a second dinner and left it on the counter, chicken and onions with enough spices that the smells of the dish permeated their neighborhood and left an indelible scent trail Cortez could follow back home. It would have worked if he hadn't been on the far side of the park.

His mother's disappointed stare bored into Cortez's head before he turned around from closing the door. When he turned to face the flames, he braced for the onslaught of heat from her words with a smile.

"I'm home," he said.

"I see that," she responded. She waited, hoping the heat would melt her son's exterior and reveal the secret he held inside. When he walked over to the counter and inspected the prepared meals—the chicken dish and the pizza, now cold—with a long sniff, she forced the issue.

"Where were you?" she said. "You never come home this late."

Cortez grabbed a plate, pretending it was the same time he arrived each day after working at the factory, and helped himself to two chicken thighs. He didn't want to lie, but he didn't see another way out of the situation. In a flash of inspiration, he told her he'd gone to a coffee shop.

"Alone?" she asked.

"No," he replied. He took his plate, sat down on the couch, and began to eat. The meat fell off the bone, and the chicken's soft tissues were indistinguishable from the flesh. "This is good," he said.

His mother ignored the compliment. "Are you going to tell me who you went with?" she said.

"I met a girl there," he said. It wasn't a lie—he had met Alara—but it wasn't the truth.

Cortez's mother changed in an instant. An angry, worried mother hen was replaced by a docile, patient bird worthy of display in an poultry show. "A girl?" she said. Never, not once, had Cortez even bothered to feign interest in the opposite sex. She had resigned herself to dying without grandkids long ago. Now, the potential continuation of her line made her look around her meager apartment, taking stock of what was suitable for children. She determined her collection of statues depicting the crucifixion were both too fragile and too violent to continue existing in the living room. A shrine for all her religious ceramics appeared in her bedroom the very next day.

Shaking herself from her daydream, his mother asked the girl's name.

"Alara," Cortez answered.

His mother spit out a rapid slew of questions. "Does she

have a last name? Where's she from? What does she do?" The questions continued for a full five minutes, without a moment for Cortez to answer a single one.

Cortez stopped eating and paid attention to her interrogation, not so he could answer her but because he realized these were the types of questions suitable for a first date. He remembered as many as he could. When his mother stopped, Cortez told her he didn't know the answer to any of them and informed her that he would find out as much as he could and report back as soon as he discovered more. The conversation inspired Cortez to come up with a few questions himself. He wanted to know whether anything she had done had caused a rainstorm, how often she worried about saying the wrong thing, and if she preferred to cry in the shower because it was an easy way to hide her tears.

"Here, let me get you more food," Cortez's mother said when she saw his empty plate. She returned with two more thighs and three tortillas. She knew, from her own experience, that children couldn't be made without the proper amount of fuel. It was the first time her son's thinness bothered her, and she resolved to remedy the situation the best way she knew how: from then on, she decided, there would be three full meals a day, and four on Sunday.

Nothing Cortez could say or do could dampen his mother's excitement at the mention of Alara. She stole glances at her son, each one bursting with maternal pride, for the entire half hour they watched television together before going to bed. When he went to bed and she reclined her seat, she stared through the ceiling, past the neighbors above her, and into the heavens, thanking God for bringing her the chance to prove her worth as a grandmother.

# CHAPTER TEN

CORTEZ WOKE up the next day with the certainty that Alara was well within his grasp. He didn't remember a single dream he'd had overnight but knew, for no reason whatsoever, that his sleeping mind had spent the previous night calculating the best way to wrest her affection away from her boyfriend. The first thing he resolved to do was to find out the name of his competition. Again, he went through the motions to keep up the appearance he was headed to the factory, but this time he was forced to eat a breakfast of four eggs and tortillas before leaving.

"You need your strength," his mother said with a twinkle in her eye. The food was swallowed down with minimal chewing.

Cortez retraced his now-familiar route back to Decant, talking to himself the entire time. While walking through the park he practiced the questions he would ask Alara, remembering a handful provided by his mother. He practiced how he would smile, how he would look at her, imagining the mannerisms of the characters on old sitcoms and hoping his own reproductions would encourage the same results. Instead of hearing the sounds of the park, he heard the laugh tracks at his jokes, the various oohs and aahs from the nonexistent studio audience. In a moment of weakness—since he knew the actors never broke the fourth wall—he waved to the trees around him, acknowledging them as if they were the imagined audience. The other people in the park who witnessed him that day never forgot the man who laughed among the trees and engaged in conversations with himself, all the while with a faraway look in his eyes, never knowing anyone else in the world existed.

Alara was working when Cortez arrived. She looked up the moment he walked in the door and gave him a nod before returning to the task at hand. Cortez believed his immense love for her had forced her to look up when he first walked in, his own body creating a magnetic field that called out to her. Even if he had been told the truth, that she was annoyed at the number of customers on that busy morning and was looking to see if there was a break in their arrival, he would have decided the strength of his love had caused the customer conditions that led to her annoyance. His love determined everything around him, the life force early philosophers tried to imbue upon everything in the world.

The line was filled with impatient people waiting for their chance to order. The lone person stationed at the register was brand new—this was her first time handling the orders without someone watching over her shoulder. To her credit, she kept her cool in spite of the angry glances from the line of people in front of her. Cortez wasn't in a rush, since he didn't have anywhere to be, but he was eager to stand opposite Alara and use some of the questions he had been practicing. He couldn't decide which one was best for the situation, and by the time he stepped to the front of the line and got his coffee—since it was the cheapest thing on the menu—no clear victor had emerged. He moved to the spot and stood opposite her, separated by the counter, and waited for her to acknowledge him.

Alara knew Cortez was in front of her, but she was too busy

to spare any energy leading him in conversation. She hoped he would move if she ignored him long enough, but it soon became clear that it wouldn't happen. She sighed, looked up, and said hello.

"Good morning, Alara," Cortez said with a smile.

The way Cortez said her name sent a chill down her spine. He said it like he knew something about her, a deep secret he kept hidden away, something he thought they shared but in fact he possessed alone. "Good morning," she said before looking back down at the next drink she had to make.

Cortez waited for divine inspiration to strike him about what to say. Instead, he was hit by the devil's jealous flame. "I saw you leaving yesterday with that guy. Is he your boyfriend?" he said. A fist-sized knot formed in his stomach, and he got the urge to crawl beneath one of the lounge chairs in the corner and die like the cockroach he was.

"Remy? Yes, he is." The look on Cortez's face was pure anguish, a tortured soul who'd just found out that his one-way ticket from hell to heaven was a fake. She loved it, which scared her. Nothing gave her more pleasure than to dash men's egos on her rocky shore, but this was different. Cortez had no ego—his presence on earth barely made a ripple—but seeing him suffer gave her great satisfaction. Unknown to her, Alara's seed of revenge had lasted for generations. Her ancestors, the Maya from the Yucatán Peninsula, had been victims of overeager missionaries, the leader of which was Cortez's ancestor. The history was lost to time, but it existed in Alara's hands, and with a cruelty she'd never experienced before she grew determined to twist the knife in the stomach of the man who stood across from her.

"It was our anniversary yesterday," she continued. Children frying an ant with a magnifying glass would be familiar with the fascination coursing through her veins. "He's a great guy. Best

I've ever met." It was a lie, but worth saying, because Cortez placed a hand on the counter for support. The truth was, Remy made it easy to be with him by paying for everything. Being treated like a decoration was something she was willing to put up with for the time being, but she'd never considered the arrangement permanent.

Cortez was struggling to breathe. The weight on his chest had increased ever since he'd asked the ill-advised question, made heavier with each word Alara spoke. He managed to hold up his coffee while mumbling something about sugar, then turned around and walked to the condiment bar so he didn't have to look at her for a second longer. Along with the belief that everything happened because of his love for her, he also believed her responses were a direct result of his poor questioning, not knowing generations of anger were being released, aimed squarely at his soul.

He spent the day lingering in Decant, getting refill after refill and attributing his beating heart to the pulses of love instead of the doses of caffeine running through his veins. Alara took the opportunity to make him squirm every time he approached, mentioning the ways Remy was a great guy, the money his family had, and the quality of his education. In truth, Alara was certain Remy would be a mediocre student if he didn't have access to the highest-quality resources. Her own parents, thinking they were doing the right thing, had kicked her out of the home as soon as she turned eighteen, forcing her to work while trying to get through school. By the time she met Cortez, the demands of both occupations had become too much, and she had dropped school to focus on working full-time. She continued reading in an attempt to further her education on her own, propelled by the desire to prove to her parents she could make it in this world. Remy's money was a benefit she didn't like to acknowledge but couldn't ignore, providing access to a way of life different from anything she had ever known.

Alara had two breaks during her seven-hour shift—a short one, ten minutes long, and a longer one so she could eat lunch. During both, she toyed around with the idea of sitting next to Cortez and continuing her torture of him. In the end, she decided to take a seat in the lobby and read. Cortez studied her while she was lost in Colombia at a time when telegraphs were still in use. The first thing he did was memorize the book she was reading: *Love in the Time of Cholera.* He deemed it fate that she was lost in a book about love; he'd never heard of cholera, pronouncing the "ch" in his head as it's written. The question he was going to ask her was seared into his brain, but the nerve to ask it never materialized. "What's your favorite book?" he imagined himself asking over and over again, in various positions and with an array of facial expressions. He'd asked it to her imagined ghost so many times, in so many ways, he forgot he had never asked the question in the first place, and when she opened the book on her second break that day he believed fate, in the form of Alara, was giving him the answer to his question by showing him the book in her hands.

He stayed for the entirety of her shift. In the late afternoon, her coworker approached her, tapped her on the shoulder, and, using one hand to point to the wrist of the other, indicated the time. Cortez had to act fast. His plan had been hatched during the hours he had watched her, and he knew that there was little time to waste. He threw away his coffee cup—along with the trash from his lunch—and closed his backpack before darting out the door, hoping Alara didn't see his quick exit. A woman with a stroller, out for a walk with her baby, almost fell victim to his hurried exit as they stood in his path. With an agility that rivaled God's winged creatures, he swerved, missing the stroller by the width of a feather. The distance between Decant and the park was covered in a handful of full-length strides as he sprinted down the street, weaving among the other people on the sidewalk. Turning, Cortez ran down the street alongside the park and dove into the shadow of the trees at the same spot he hoped Alara would enter within minutes.

His plan was simple: to wait for Alara at her favorite bench.

ALARA's favorite bench had seen better times. It was made of wood riddled with wounds from the spaces left by large splinters. Some of the trenches were the same color as the bench itself, and the fresher wounds were the light brown of new wood. A trash can nearby overflowed with plastic bags and various colored wrappers, and there were water bottles placed along the rim, some of which had fallen onto the surrounding grass. Cortez took a seat and watched the soccer game taking place in the open grassy space ahead of him, nervous at the prospect of sitting next to Alara. His list of prepared questions swirled through his head. Determined to ask one that would lead to a more fruitful conversation, he decided to ask about the book she was reading; he knew the title but little else. He stared ahead, lost in thought, while the team without shirts scored.

Alara laughed to herself when she saw Cortez seated in her spot. She considered finding another spot to read before he saw her, not wanting to share her space, but instead she exhaled and emerged from beneath the trees, walking straight to where she planned to spend the rest of the winding-down afternoon. There was no way she would allow him to rain on her parade, not when she'd spent all day cooped up indoors and craved the sunshine. When she got close, Cortez turned and looked at her. He looked both scared and fascinated, making her feel like a beautiful, poisonous creature. She sat down and kept her eyes straight ahead, aware that Cortez was staring at her.

The silence tore Cortez apart. He couldn't command his tongue to speak words and for the first time came to hate his body, a repulsion that separated his mind from his flesh. The split never healed.

"You've followed me before, haven't you," she said after a moment had passed. She was not aware of Cortez's inner turmoil.

Cortez knew he had to say something. He didn't want to acknowledge her question, hoping that ignoring it would erase his duplicitous actions. It occurred to him that she must not know about him following her home, a fact that provided little relief from the flames surrounding him. He mustered every ounce of strength he had and asked, "What book are you reading?" though he already knew the answer.

Alara withdrew her book and showed him the cover. "This is my third time reading it. He's my favorite author."

Cortez was elated at the correctness of his instincts, making no distinction between favorite author and favorite book. He had never heard of Gabriel García Márquez, but he decided then and there to find out as much as he could about him. Alara turned to face him before he could think of a response.

"Leave me alone so I can read," she said.

Cortez scurried away, knowing he had just gotten a glimpse of the lock around her heart, and certain he knew the exact place where he could find the key.

THE SATURDAY after he learned Alara's literary preferences was unlike any Cortez had ever known. He leapt from his bed at the same time he did during the week, this time without an alarm, because he hadn't slept the night before. His night had been spent in the hazy half-light of darkness familiar to those who live in the city, his eyes wide open and staring at the ceiling, certain that no dream could be as comforting as the memory of sitting next to Alara the previous day. Saturdays were his chance to sleep late each week, instead of waking up to go to work or church, and his habit was to transplant himself from the bed to the couch and watch television until it was lunchtime. Not having slept a wink, he abandoned the task, eager to put the plan that had kept him awake all night into action.

His mother was still in her room when he got ready for the day, and he ate some of the leftovers overflowing from their refrigerator that had appeared after he shared there was a woman in his life. He closed their front door, careful not to make a noise, and descended the building's steps. The world outside his apartment had been awaiting his arrival. Birds launched from their perch and flew in clusters of ever-changing shapes, calling out to each other through the cloud-free sky. His neighbors, who ignored him most days, went out of their way to say hello. Each step he took was lighter than the one before, and by the time he got to the library he was floating on a pad of air as thick as the Bible.

# CHAPTER ELEVEN

A FIELD TRIP had introduced Cortez to the public library when he was in elementary school. The teachers and librarians had teamed up to provide every student with a library card, one that Cortez still kept, with pride, in his wallet next to his identification card and whatever cash he carried, when he had it. The occasion to use the card again had never emerged until now.

The library was a single-story old building made of bricks stained green from moss, with a metal roof with peeling red paint. An extraordinary amount of wires ran to the building from a nearby telephone pole, all connected to a single pole of Cortez's height perched at the building's corner. None of the wires were active. The operational telephone lines and electricity grid were all connected via underground cables, but since none of the workers who had laid the new infrastructure were told to get rid of the previous iterations, nobody did. Black birds of various sizes perched on the wires throughout the day, leaving a thick line of their droppings on the path beneath them. The library's few windows were reinforced with metal grates, protection from book thieves that never materialized.

Cortez pulled on the front door and found it locked. He

cupped his hands over his eyes and leaned forward, peering into the small vertical window. It was deserted, but not empty; leaning stacks of books were piled on every surface. His arm brushed against a laminated piece of paper taped to the front door that he hadn't noticed before.

THIS LOCATION CLOSED ON WEEKENDS. CITY'S MAIN LIBRARY (ACROSS THE PARK) OPEN 7 DAYS A WEEK.

So, for yet another time, Cortez set off across the park. He couldn't stay away from the other side of the city, a fact that he took as a sign he was meant to be with Alara Chel. Going to the library on the other side of the city allowed him to be closer to her, which added more fuel to the fire raging inside him, more strength to complete the day's mission. His feet returned to earth when he arrived on the other side of the park, at the moment he realized he had to ask for directions because he had no idea where the library was located. After he was ignored twice, a wrinkled woman rolling a basket full of groceries with small steps pointed in the opposite direction of Decant. He considered going to the coffee shop to see if Alara was working but decided he needed to be prepared for the next time they met, preparation he hoped would be complete by the end of the day, so he followed the woman's finger until he arrived at his destination.

The library held the key to Cortez's future. The building took up an entire block. It was built to stand for generations, a secure repository of the world's knowledge that the city's inhabitants could access every day of the week. Her sibling, the courthouse, stood blocks away; they were twin pillars holding up the virtues of the city. Dozens of wide stone steps rose from the sidewalk to the columns that ended beneath ornate carvings of books, dates, and animals, none of which were particular to the library but were there for decoration—the courthouse displayed similar images. Cortez found the entrance repugnant, an ostentatious display of power humble books didn't require. Despite his distaste, he climbed the front steps, walked through the columns, and went past the open dark-wood doors. A new world awaited him inside.

Multiple tables were set up, each overseen by an adult with a bright orange T-shirt. They were responsible for the hordes of children walking around the space, most with an adult close at hand but some roaming free. There were balloons, smiles, and books littered throughout. Cortez had never seen so many pencils; they were pre-sharpened and sitting in cups at the tables, ready to be taken by children along with accompanying index cards or forms for the children to fill out. On the far side of the lobby, past the bazaar, was a vast staircase that started wide and narrowed at the top with stacks of books visible beyond. The railings on each side were green, accented with brass, and prevented people from falling down into the aisles on either side of the staircase, where there were rooms with more book stacks.

There had never been many children in Cortez's adult life, and for the most part he deemed them frivolous. But that day, seeing the eagerness of their quest for knowledge, he smiled, wondering how his own life would be different if he'd been infected with their same sickness when he was young. He left the festival behind and walked up the staircase, ready to plunge headfirst into the pages. Vertigo took him in her clutches when he saw the magnitude of his task. The stacks went off far into the distance. With the name of Alara's book in his mind, he began walking around, trusting the divine would point him in the right direction. A few minutes went by without a single title registering in his mind, forcing him to walk back and begin once more. He passed a staircase with arrows that informed him there were more books on the levels above and below his current location, a revelation that made him stumble from the enormity of his task.

A librarian noticed the somber young man in her domain when he walked past twice without acknowledging her presence. Her glasses were green and pointed at the corners, connected by a chain of green beads around her neck, and they gave her an insect's appearance. Bushy red hair matched the shawl she insisted on wearing each day because she got cold and was scared of getting sick, one she left behind in the library each night when she got off work. It hadn't left the premises in years, even to be washed. When the searcher passed her for a third time, she cleared her throat.

"Looking for something, young man?" she said to get his attention.

"A book," Cortez responded.

The librarian first chuckled, then grew frustrated when she realized it wasn't meant as a joke. "Which book?" she said.

"It's called *Love in Time for Cholera*," Cortez said. He mispronounced the last word.

The librarian was taken aback by the patron's certainty, even though she knew the exact title he was looking for. "You mean: *Love in the Time of* Cholera," she corrected him, making sure to accentuate the correct pronunciation of the sickness.

"Yes, I think that's the one. Do you have it?" Cortez said.

"Follow me," the librarian said. She led Cortez through a series of twists and turns he couldn't have reproduced even if he had made an attempt to memorize the sequence. While walking, she tried to bring him out of his shell, treating him like other introverts who suffered from a love of books. "It's a wonderful book . . . he's a renowned author . . . one of the best love stories ever told . . ." None of her attempts at conversation had the desired effect.

She found the book, pulled it from the shelf, and handed it

to him. "You can check it out at the front desk," she informed him.

"Good to know, but I need to finish it today," Cortez said without a trace of humility. The truth was, he hadn't read a complete book since the last time he'd finished a picture book with his mother as a child. "Is there somewhere I can sit and read right now?"

The librarian tilted her head forward and looked at him from above the rim of her glasses. "Right over there," she said, pointing to the far side of the room. "Each floor has a dedicated reading area overlooking the park. It's what we're famous for," she said with pride.

Cortez thanked her before walking away. The librarian shook her head, thinking to herself that she had a lot to learn. She'd seen all kinds of God's creatures before, and it would have never crossed her mind that the young man she'd helped was the type to read an entire novel in a day.

The book was thicker than Cortez's Bible. The larger font was little consolation, because he'd never read anything more than the handful of passages he'd memorized. By the end of the first page he was beginning to lose steam, and after reading the first four pages not a single word registered in his love-addled mind. The words didn't go in and slip from his grasp; they never went in at all. The book in Cortez's hands kept lowering as if it was sinking through water, each time retrieved from the depths with renewed focus when he jolted awake. His ability to concentrate waned as his eyelids grew heavier, and soon after he turned the fifth page he fell into a deep sleep, his body starving after staying awake the night before.

HE WAS SHAKEN awake by what he assumed was an angel. She didn't have the same effect on him as Alara—no woman could—

but the haze around her blond hair and soft smile made him wonder how long until he met Peter.

"Tell him he can't sleep here!" Cortez heard the librarian with insect eyes say in the distance.

The young blond librarian closed her eyes and shook her head. "Don't worry about her. She's probably just cold." In the distance, the woman pulled the shawl tighter around her shoulders. "What are you reading?"

Cortez showed her the cover of the book. A page had bent when he was asleep. "Sorry about that," he said with a sheepish grin.

"Our little secret," the woman said with a wink, holding out a hand to take the book from him.

"I've got to finish it today," Cortez continued, maintaining his hold on the book.

"Why? What happens if you don't?"

Cortez grew embarrassed at the thought of divulging his secret. "It's for a friend," he stammered.

"You're reading an entire book in a day for a friend?" she exclaimed. "You're a good friend," she added. She indicated to Cortez that he had something on his face, below his lips.

Cortez used the back of his arm to wipe drool from his chin.

"Did you know they made this into a movie? It might be easier than reading the book."

Cortez's heart leapt at his sudden stroke of fortune. "They did? Do you know where I can get it?" Remembering he didn't have enough money with him to buy a movie, he realized he'd have to go home first.

"We have a copy here," the librarian informed him. She thought he was cute when the smile erased the melancholy from his face.

"Is there somewhere I can watch it?" he asked, timid. He didn't want his mother to ask why he was watching that particular movie. She was aware of Alara, yes, but she didn't need to know his plan.

"Here? Let's go find out." This time, Cortez handed over the book when she extended her arm.

The young woman led Cortez to the station she shared with the librarian whose shawl protected her from freezing to death. "Would it be possible to set him up in one of the private rooms upstairs?" she asked her colleague.

The frozen woman looked at her younger counterpart in shock. "No way, that's for educational purposes only."

"This is a library, Gert. Everything we do is educational." She rolled her eyes and looked at Cortez. "Could you give us a second?" she said, pointing to the side. Cortez waited a few steps away. Minutes later, the kind librarian led Cortez to another part of the library, talking the entire time.

"She's nice, once you get to know her," she said. They were among bookcases filled with DVDs. She found the one she was looking for, handed it to Cortez to carry, then led him to the staircase.

"The private rooms are on the top floor."

They climbed four flights of stairs and emerged in a shadowy corridor that had dark rooms along the entirety of its length. "These aren't used very often, so I don't know why she had to make a big deal of you using one."

The librarian opened the door closest to them—it was unlocked—turned on the lights, and ushered Cortez inside. It was small, wide enough for a single table surrounded by four chairs, and had an ancient television strapped onto a rolling cart with a DVD player beneath. She told Cortez to sit down and got the movie ready to watch.

"When you're done, do me a favor and turn everything off, including the lights, then just come down and find me. I'll be at the same station."

Cortez nodded, and she pressed play before leaving him alone, closing the door behind her. For the next two hours and nineteen minutes, he watched, enraptured. It didn't take long for him to realize his role in the love triangle. His destiny, like that of Florentino Ariza, was to wait, and he resigned himself to take up the sacred suffering with as much seriousness as he accepted the body and blood of Christ on Sundays. He grew to hate Dr. Juvenal Urbino for taking so long to die. When the movie ended, he was imbued with the certainty that Alara needed saving from Remy, more so than Fermina Daza needed saving from Urbino, because while their story had already been told, Alara's was just now being written.

THE LIBRARIANS WERE CHATTING while working through a stack of books on the counter in front of them. As Cortez approached, the temperature dropped a few degrees, and both women's arms were covered in goosebumps. His smile chilled them to the bone, freezing what little flesh had still been left intact.

"All done," he said, holding out the movie. The disc was covered with large red flowers visible through the clear plastic protective covering. When Cortez saw the bright petals in the well-lit part of the library, he grew certain he knew where to find the source of Alara's smell, the one he'd dreamt about two nights before. He'd smell every flower on earth if he had to, just to find the one that belonged to her.

The young librarian took it from his hands and smiled back, a brave attempt at normalcy in spite of the elements. "How did you like it?"

The bundled-up librarian was impressed by her colleague's ability to maintain cordiality while speaking to the strange visitor, and from then on never second-guessed any of her decisions.

"It was wonderful," Cortez said. "Best I've seen."

"I'm glad to hear it. Anything else we can help you with?"

"There is. Do you know of any gardens around here?"

She thought for a moment. "I think there's one in the park. Gert, do you know?"

Gertrude, looking at Cortez through her green glasses, would have said anything to get him out of the library and away from her. She told Cortez about the park's botanical gardens and where to find them. "Have a great time," she said, the last word clipped by a clack of her teeth.

"I will," he said, with a serpentine smile, before walking back out into the world.

# CHAPTER TWELVE

Cortez had to continue in the opposite direction of Decant, aware that it was away from Alara, in order to get to the park's garden. It was surrounded by a dark gray chest-high barrier that absorbed the sunlight, with a taller wrought iron gate that served as an entrance. The people entering and leaving the garden were the relaxed sort who were out for an afternoon stroll, content with experiencing nature; they didn't pay attention to the feverish soul who joined them. Cortez walked in with the determination of a prisoner who had just learned his sentence and didn't want to give the judge the satisfaction of seeing him suffer. He walked past the examples of various trees, each one with a sign in front informing readers of the scientific name and characteristics typical of the species, and made his way to the section of flowers in the back. Alara's vapors reached him during a long whiff, one of many smells that filtered in through his nose. He got to work identifying hers, as if he was scanning a crowd for the one face that belonged to his beloved.

The faint sweetness of tulips didn't possess her vitality, and the hydrangeas were too heavy to belong to the lightness of her footsteps. He narrowed it down to the orchids, for they reminded him of her femininity, and the carnations, because their smell surrounded him the same way her memory did when he wasn't in her presence. Going back and forth between the two flowers, he became convinced he needed to mix them together to find the perfect concoction. Looking around to make sure he was alone before plucking a flower from each plant, he noticed a bush of red roses in the garden's corner. Not wanting to leave a stone unturned, he approached, leaned forward, and sniffed. The scent transported him away from reality, back into his dreams, and he stood tall, certain he had stepped outside of time. It was her smell. He wanted to lie in it, roll in it, bathe in it, and live in it. With nobody around him, he reached forward and tried to pluck the largest flower, not having seen the thorn hidden beneath the petals. It stuck deep in his thumb. He pulled his hand away and stared at the blood.

He had bled for her. To him, nothing was more sacred than suffering for the one he loved, for he knew Jesus had suffered on the cross for his beloved earth creatures. He licked the blood away and stared at the hole in his thumb. It was time for him to accept the crown of thorns. After lifting the rose petals and locating the largest thorn, he stuck it through his thumb until it hit the nail on the other side. He was smiling the entire time. The pain brought him closer to Alara, and he imagined she was on top of him with her hair, smelling of roses, surrounding his face.

Cortez pulled his thumb away and positioned his body between the lone rose bush and the rest of the garden before snapping the rose from the stalk. The other plants didn't need to know he was complicit in the destruction of their brethren, and he preferred to keep this secret from them so their flowers wouldn't seek revenge and cause his sinuses to revolt in the future.

The afternoon sun cast the shadows of the longest buildings

far into the park. Cortez left the garden with the souvenir of his visit in his pocket. As he passed walkers, sunbathers, and exercisers, he put his hand into his pocket, squeezed the petals, then sniffed his fingers. His thumb was still bleeding, and every so often he sucked the blood from the tip. He didn't know where he was going and couldn't think long enough to come to a decision, because every time the scent he associated with Alara hit his nostrils he became disoriented, lost in a dream. Step after step he approached her part of the city, and soon he plunged into the shadows that covered the sidewalks, the sun hidden by the buildings on each side.

His legs took him to Decant. He stood outside the front window, looking inside. Alara was behind the counter, unaware she was being watched. Cortez squeezed the rose in his pocket so tightly that when he withdrew his hand it was covered in red. He stared at his palm then put his hand back in his pocket. She would have to wait.

Remy's apartment wasn't far. It took Cortez a few tries to remember which block he lived on, but once he did, he leaned against the building across the street. According to the movie, he had to wait until Remy died. Cortez was driven by curiosity; he wanted to know more about the man, to know his lifestyle and habits, so he could have some idea of how long he might be stuck in purgatory. There was no plan other than to be in close proximity—murdering Alara's boyfriend had never crossed his mind. The heat of Remy's presence brought his hatred to a boil. Cortez stayed there until well after the sun went down.

On the opposite side of the city, Cortez's mother grew worried. For the last few weeks, they had spent Saturday nights out on the town, searching for lost souls to save. The people spending money, eating like kings, the fornicators: they all were worthy candidates to receive Christ's love. Both Cortez and his mother had no friends, and therefore no social obligations, and their evangelizing was the perfect use of their weekend night. A way to rush their salvation by growing the size of the Church, even though their fishing had been unsuccessful to that point. The lunch his mother had made earlier, chorizo and beans, was sitting in the refrigerator on a paper plate. Since Cortez never came home, she hadn't made dinner. At first, she assumed he was with the girl. Now, with the coming of the storm clouds in the distance, she wondered if he was all right, if he was safe, and she kicked herself for not asking more questions when he first mentioned his new preoccupation. She knew women made men do stupid things, but she had no idea what kind of trouble her son was capable of finding.

REMY APPEARED after the rain started. His broad shoulders and soldier-straight back made him easy to recognize. He had a black umbrella in his hand and was dressed in dark slacks, dress shoes, and a light blue button-up shirt. The light drizzle never reached his umbrella, the rain altering its path to avoid him. He set off down the street, taking long strides that cleared the puddles in his path.

Cortez didn't have the same power over the elements. In fact, he had the opposite effect. Instead of a light rain, he walked through a downpour as he followed Remy. Nothing was going to stop his pursuit. Curiosity about the man he had come to hate outweighed anything the world might throw at him. Block after block Cortez followed him. They passed by the fountain where Cortez had watched him dine with Alara. Remy continued until he got to a row of sports bars, where he went inside one without hesitation.

The bar Remy entered was one of five on the same block. They were notorious for being frequented by the city's younger inhabitants, most college-aged or within a few years of graduation. There was an Irish bar, a cowboy-themed bar, and a bar with a horse statue in front. None of the bars had windows separating their interiors from the street outside. Raucous noise spilled out of each, sports games and shouts Cortez thought had no place at dinnertime. Cortez had never seen so many people his own age concentrated in one area before, and the sight of them was another distraction from the hunger he had never gotten around to noticing. Even if he had, the establishments didn't serve anything but greasy bar food and numerous specials based on various mixtures of liquor and beer.

The crowd made it easy for Cortez to stay hidden while he watched Remy after following him inside. The young man was with three friends, the four of them cheering for the soccer team on the screen behind the bar. Cortez knew nothing of sports and made a mental note to ask Alara her thoughts on them. Since she wasn't there, he assumed she didn't like them either, and not watching them could be an interest they both shared. The back wall soon became Cortez's best friend. He was close enough to the bathroom that people would ask if he was in line, and each time he shook his head no and looked past the questioner, they stared at the young man who looked so out of place and miserable in his own skin.

A young woman, wearing a skirt and with a dizzy look in her eyes, leaned on the wall next to Cortez. It was obvious she had been drinking all day. Cortez ignored her. She asked him what his name was and he didn't respond. Not to be deterred, she said it again, louder.

"What's your name?"

There was no way Cortez could pretend not to hear. He looked at her and sized her up. "Cortez," he said, turning back towards where Remy sat at the bar.

The drunk woman leaned forward and whispered into Cortez's ear. "My name's Olivia."

Cortez pulled his head away. "That's nice."

One of Remy's friends stood up, turned around, and walked right towards Cortez. A momentary panic set in, one in which he wondered if Remy had sent his friend to confront Cortez. When the friend walked right by Cortez and into the bathroom, Cortez moved away, thanking God for sending him a sign to get out of the way before Remy's inevitable use of the restroom. The drunk woman, having decided she wanted to know more about Cortez, followed him to his new perch.

"Where's your drink?" she slurred.

Cortez told her he didn't drink in the most serious voice he possessed.

"Really? Then what are you doing here?"

Cortez looked at her. "I'm watching the game. What are you doing here?"

She looked at the television above the bar. "Me too, me too," she said. Together, they watched the game, until something distracted her and Cortez was left alone once more. He squeezed the rose in his pocket, whispering thanks for the inspired presence of Alara's ghost at his side.

REMY WENT to the bathroom when the game ended, unaware his every move was being watched. Cortez thought he'd be leaving the bar now that the game was over, but the energy of the people in the bar was escalating instead of dying down. Remy ordered shots when he went back to his friends. Cortez looked around himself in disgust. The people were sweaty, drunk, and touching each other way too much. Their behavior hadn't been so bad when he first got there, and their steady decline was never visible when viewed moment by moment, but now that he recognized it, he couldn't believe there were people who chose to participate in the debauchery. He thought about his plan to attend church the next day, about finding people who would join him in worship, and for the first time he understood what his mother had said about God not wanting "those kinds of people." His mother's expectation about their Saturday night activity never crossed his mind because, for him, it hadn't been a regular enough occurrence to be considered a part of his routine.

The second woman who approached him reinforced his opinion of the situation. Hours had gone by, and Remy had shown no signs of leaving. Cortez was standing still, ever vigilant, not wanting to miss any of Alara's boyfriend's actions, when the woman appeared in his vicinity. She was younger and drunker than the others, with red blemishes on her face and evidence of spilled liquid down the front of her green dress. Her black boots went up to just below her knees and were well-worn in a way that suggested her foot's heel didn't align with the heel of the boot when she walked.

"You're cute," she said. She stumbled against the wall next to him.

"Thanks," said Cortez. He was getting tired. His eyelids were held open through sheer willpower. He had never been called cute before, but since the compliment didn't come from Alara, he didn't care.

The girl's eyelids were held open just enough to make sure she didn't fall over. The whites of her eyes, streaked with red, were hard to distinguish. "Do you live close to here?" she said.

"Why?" Cortez said, defensive. He was confused, wondering if she could tell he was from the other part of the city by the way he dressed, how he stood, or some other characteristic he wasn't aware he possessed.

"Because I can come over and spend the night," she said, planting a wet kiss on his neck.

Cortez's heart raced at the thought of spending the night

with her. He had never been with a woman before, and he grew worried doing so would poison his knight's devotion to Alara. The repercussions of the action on his soul's ability to enter heaven never crossed his mind. Even God went to sleep past a certain point in the night, leaving his children to fend for themselves.

"That isn't going to happen," Cortez told her. "I'm taken." Cortez put his hand over his mouth and nose and inhaled the scent of roses. Somehow, he could still find the scent among the stale beer and sweat.

"Then what are you doing in a bar so late at night?" she said before walking away.

Cortez looked for Remy, wondering the same thing. It was past midnight, and Remy had been turning down women all night. He drank, but not enough to lose control of his senses. When Cortez looked back at the spot on the bar that had belonged to his target, the man had disappeared. A pit grew in Cortez's stomach, fearful his position had been discovered, and he examined his immediate surroundings. Remy wasn't close by. Relief washed over him, and Cortez broadened his search, finding his target walking out the front door with a beautiful girl under one arm. She was blond, thin, and used to being the prettiest girl in any room she entered.

The rain had stopped during their hours in the bar and Remy, no longer needing it, had forgotten his umbrella under the bar. Cortez knew but wasn't going to be the one to tell him. He walked behind the drunk couple as they retraced the path back to Remy's apartment, finding ways to touch each other while they walked. They would hold hands, then Remy would put an arm around her. Three separate times they ducked into the sunken threshold of a store and made out.

A pang of guilt ran through Cortez each time the couple disappeared from view, as if he was the one cheating on Alara.

He had to spit into the street multiple times to get the taste of bile from his mouth, thankful the street was already wet because of the rain. His body was exhausted, but he willed it forward with the stubbornness of a mule, certain this was the reason he had been called to follow Remy in the first place. High above them the sky was pitch black, but down on the streets the lights from the streetlamps illuminated every one of Remy's actions, and Cortez was certain God wanted him to see so he could test the strength of his devotion to patience.

Remy and his companion turned the corner a block ahead. Cortez maintained his pace, knowing they would be in the distance when he turned onto the new block himself. His eyes took the opportunity to shut, letting Cortez walk blind while they didn't have to keep the couple in sight. They commanded his hand to brush along the length of the building, promising to open when the hand detected open air. The building was rough stone and scraped his palm. At the building's corner, Cortez turned and his eyes opened. There, right in front of his face at the corner, stood Remy and the girl.

# CHAPTER THIRTEEN

THE COUPLE WAS WAITING in line for a slice of pizza when Cortez appeared next to them. The small restaurant was famous for how late they served their signature dish, and at this time of night there was nothing else open. Even if there were other places to get food, the pizza was a tradition, the best way to cap off the night. It was the way Remy had gotten the blond girl to leave the bar with him, a trick he had used numerous times before. The restaurant was close to his apartment, and he then offered a space to eat the late-night meal. Once they were alone in his apartment, he could work his magic. His system didn't account for being followed.

It was hard to determine who was more surprised: Remy, Cortez, or Liza. She had met Remy for the first time that night and thought he was handsome. When he paid her tab and offered to buy her pizza, she accepted, even though she hadn't drank enough to make a bad decision. It wasn't like her to go off with new men on any night, let alone when she was still in full control of herself, but something about his confidence had convinced her to give him a chance. She wasn't disappointed, and soon found herself enjoying whispered conversations in shadowy corners along their walk, quick discussions that ended with his lips on hers.

"You followed us," Remy said when he saw Cortez. It wasn't said with an overwhelming amount of anger—which Liza would have thought off-putting—but as a declaration of fact, as if her new friend was prepared to fight for her honor.

Liza put a hand on his chest. "I have no idea who he is," she said. Men had followed her before. They had never been dangerous and convinced her they only wanted to talk. But the risk of being stalked was always present, which was why she never went anywhere alone.

Remy looked at the blond girl with sober eyes. His sobriety infected her, removing her sense of well-being and bringing her world into focus. "Why would you?" he said.

She pulled his hand from her chest. "I don't know," she said. She looked at the object of Remy's wrath. He was thin, his face sallow, and he was terrified. As she watched, Cortez put his hand into his pocket then withdrew it, holding it up to his face and taking a whiff that brought all the air in the city into his nostrils. His ritual transformed him, and he looked at Remy with a murderous stare.

Before Liza knew what was happening, Remy had left her side. He walked right up to Cortez and punched him in the stomach. Cortez doubled over but, to Liza's surprise, stood standing.

"Stop." A punch to the side. "Following." A pull on the shoulder, bringing Cortez to standing. "Me!" A punch to the face, accompanied by a sickening crunch of bones.

Cortez couldn't stay standing through the second onslaught. The crowd, who a moment before had been waiting for pizza, had made a circle around the two men and witnessed the beating. They parted when Remy took Liza with him to the front of the line, ordered two slices, and paid for them with a large bill, telling the employees to forget they saw anything in exchange for the massive tip.

A member of the crowd helped Cortez sit up. Another one went inside for water. Blood was pouring from Cortez's nose, and he couldn't breathe without a sharp pain in his side. "Are you OK?" the person helping him sit up asked. Cortez struggled to make out the brown beard that took up most of the man's face. The man held up two fingers.

"How many fingers am I holding up?"

Cortez turned away. "It doesn't matter," he muttered.

"That only works in movies, Ronnie," Ronnie's friend said from the crowd.

Two cups of water appeared in front of Cortez. He used them, along with a copious amount of accompanying napkins, to wipe as much blood as he could from his face. Cortez smiled when he realized how much blood he'd spilled that day in pursuit of Alara.

Liza looked back as she walked away with Remy after getting their slices. They wouldn't be followed anymore, that was for certain. She was also quite sure she'd imagined the terrified face, because now the victim of the beating looked delighted.

"Did that guy just attack you for no reason?" Ronnie, the one with the beard, asked while Cortez was struggling to stand up.

Cortez stood tall. "He has a reason," he said, laughing. "I'm going to take his girl."

As Cortez walked home, the pain in his side increased until he had trouble standing up straight. Every breath took an extraordinary amount of willpower to complete. He couldn't breathe through his swollen nose, and every swallow brought with it an awareness of his loose front teeth and the dull ache in his jaw. The employees had offered him a slice of pizza on the house, but he'd refused because he didn't think he could eat anything without losing a tooth. His maniacal laughter had died away when he left the crowd behind, leaving him gloomy, sore, and aware of how alone he was in the world. Walking through the park left him with an icy chill, and the one thing that kept him marching forward was the thought of his warm bed.

Being on his side of the city, in a familiar place, provided a measure of comfort. He knew to avoid the groups huddled in front of apartments, to keep his head down and ignore their jeers. Each of the two bucket fires he passed were surrounded by people either lying down or sitting at the edges of the provided glow. Nobody would have stopped him from warming his hands in front of the fires, a fellow night creature in need of their resource, but he kept moving, urged by his home's call.

His mother stood in front of their apartment building. She was like a lighthouse in a storm, her eyes scanning the horizon in every direction, looking for her son to emerge through the ocean's mist. When he hobbled up to her, the pain in his side affecting his gait, she rushed out to meet him, her mother's instincts on full alert. She didn't hug him, aware the pressure of her arms might crush what little strength he had left. Instead, she held his shoulders and kept him at arm's length, inspecting him. There was enough artificial light from the surrounding buildings for her to get a sense of the damage to his face.

"What happened to you?" she exclaimed. Cortez had never been a rambunctious child. There were no broken bones or stitches in his past. She doubted he'd ever even suffered a paper cut. Seeing his blood was one of the great fears of her life, and she always wondered how she would handle a situation when it emerged. From then on, she was always proud she had kept her composure in the moment she first saw him bleed, looking for a practical solution instead of growing faint at the sight of her son's condition.

"Nothing," Cortez said. He shrugged her away, trying to continue on his death march to his resting place. His mother could be dealt with tomorrow.

She wasn't willing to let him go. One hand on Cortez's shoulder twisted him back around, flooding his senses with the memory of Remy the moment before he had been struck in the face. His hands went up out of pure instinct. His mother let go and stepped back, horrified that he was scared of her.

"I would never," she said. Her eyes welled with tears.

Cortez dropped his hands and took a deep breath to steady his nerves. His mother was struck by how much time had passed from when he was still her little boy.

"I know," Cortez said. "It's been a long night. Can we just go upstairs?"

"Not until you tell me where you've been. I was worried all night! Do you think I like being up this late, standing outside, waiting for you to come home?"

"You could have stayed upstairs," Cortez said.

"I was going crazy upstairs," his mother whispered. Her moment of weakness, born from the fear she'd had to live with not knowing if her son was safe, or even alive, didn't pass unnoticed by Cortez. He closed his eyes and told her the truth.

"Alara's friend beat me up," Cortez said.

"Does he want to take her from you?" his mother asked. In her mind, Cortez was the crown jewel, the prince, and she couldn't imagine a world where a woman didn't recognize his greatness.

"Something like that." A tear slid down his cheek, a single drop of frustration, embarrassment, and pain.

"Let's go upstairs," his mother said. "You can tell me more when we're inside."

Cortez's mother stood behind him while they climbed the stairs. His reserve strength was depleted, and they had to stop multiple times before making it up the seven flights. She had never seen her son in such a vulnerable state, and she worried about what deed of her own had caused this situation to occur. Both mother and son shared the same unshaken belief that the world around them was the result of their own actions. It was an inherited delusion, passed down from generations, that caused each of them to carry the weight of the world on their shoulders. It wasn't a shared weight; they each possessed their own separate world.

CORTEZ GOT to the apartment first and found the door locked. He peeled himself away from the threshold and gave his mother space to access the lock.

"I don't have my key," he said. He kicked himself for forgetting, heaping more pain on his already fragile body.

At those words, his mother knew she had made a mistake. "I don't have my key either." She tried turning the lock herself. "It shouldn't be locked."

This one stumbling block was too much for Cortez. He leaned his back against the wall and collapsed in a heap. "I just want to be left alone." He pulled his knees to his chest, as close as he could without causing too much pain, then rested his forehead on them. His tears rushed out, and at the same moment the rain outside began again. It pelted against the window at the end of the hall, and down on the streets the downpour extinguished the bucket fires, causing everyone relying on their light and heat to scatter in search of cover.

His mother sat down next to him. "Why did her friend beat you up?"

Cortez started talking into his lap, telling his mother how he had met Alara at the coffee shop, about the free drink he'd received from her and their time spent on a bench discussing literature. He told her about walking Alara home, and about seeing her leave to spend time with a friend.

"This woman is leading you on, my son," his mother said when he finished his tale, tapping his shin three times.

Cortez lifted his face and looked at his mother with eyes so full of anguish it crippled her ability to enjoy romantic movies ever again. "Doesn't she know I just want to make her happy?"

His mother extended an arm around him and held him close. She ran her fingers through his hair, happy to be the one to console him. He was her independent boy, the one who always brushed off the world around him, and feeling needed, which she hadn't felt since he was a small child, was worth staying up late and getting locked out of her home.

"That woman doesn't deserve you," she said.

In an instant, Cortez transformed from her son into a viper. He pulled himself away, wiped his tears, and glared at her, ready to strike. "Don't talk about her like that," he said.

"She doesn't! You're all love, and she's throwing you to the wolves." They both stood up.

"You don't know the first thing about her," Cortez hissed.

"I know she's a fool of a woman."

Cortez looked at his mother. He wanted her to hurt. It was the first time he realized it was possible to share the weight on his shoulders, and he tried to share the entirety of his load with her. "You don't know the first thing about love," he managed to sputter. He never knew why he started with that statement, but it was the first crack in the dam before the water came rushing out.

Lightning illuminated the sky outside the window. "I love you," she said. The accompanying thunder shook the building down to its foundation.

"You can't keep anyone by your side who doesn't have to be there," Cortez spat out. Releasing his venom was like learning to walk for the first time; infinite possibilities awaited him in the world. "It's why dad left. He didn't have to be here anymore, so he took the first chance he got to leave."

"You're hurting," his mother said, wiping the tears from her eyes. "You don't mean what you say."

"I mean it!" Cortez roared. His proclamation woke the neighbors. Every door on their floor opened and faces emerged, looking for the source of the commotion. The neighbors shook their heads before going back to bed, not because of the yelling itself, but because it wasn't scheduled. Everyone thanked their lucky stars Ms. Roberts didn't have a male guest over that night.

"I have to stay here because I have nowhere else to go. Have you ever asked yourself if I really love you, or if I'm just stuck?"

Cortez's mother let her gaze fall to the floor. This venomous creature wasn't her son. The image of the boy she held on to with the iron grip of rigor mortis slipped away, replaced by an awareness of the full-grown man ahead of her. A man who didn't know his limitations, who was still stuck in the delusions of an adolescent. She lifted her eyes and stared at him, seeing what he had become for the first time.

"Why do you think you have nowhere else to go?" his mother asked.

The coldness of her tone dulled Cortez's fangs and transformed them back to human teeth. He sensed he had overplayed his hand, but he was committed to seeing his maneuvers through, even if that meant his own welcome destruction. He stayed silent while his mother widened her eyes and jutted her face towards him.

"Hm?" she said. When Cortez didn't respond, she continued. "I'm not keeping you hostage. I've never once told you not to leave. Since you know everything, why don't you tell me why you have nowhere else to go?"

Cortez was shrinking. At the height of his rage, his head had tickled the ceiling. Now, he was eye level with the door handle. He wished his mother would bring the guillotine down on his neck and end the torture. The rain continued to flood the city streets.

"Because no one loves me," Cortez answered. The admission released some of his pain into the world, creating room for more.

"Nobody but me. But keep going. Why do you think that is?"

By now, Cortez was the size of an insect. Animal instinct urged him to scurry away, to find a split in the wall where he could hide in darkness, but he was frozen to the spot. He stared at his mother, pleading with her to bring her foot down and put an end to his miserable existence. She didn't give him the satisfaction. Instead, she opened his eyes and showed him the fibers of the carpet his insect legs carried him through, a much worse punishment than the quick, painless death of being crushed.

"It's because you're not *normal*," she said when he didn't answer. "Who's going to put up with you and your ridiculous routines? Me. Who's going to make sure you have food you like to eat? Me. You think I don't want to eat eggplant? I love eggplant! But, since you don't, guess who never has eggplant. Us!"

Cortez didn't understand how routines were difficult—didn't it mean he was reliable? And he had never once asked her to make any type of food; she chose to do so under her own free will. Every complaint his mother had against him came out in a torrent of words that rivaled the water overflowing the sewers outside. She gained momentum as she spoke.

"Nobody else can love you because you're unlovable. Who

wants to live in fear of spilling toothpaste on the bathroom counter because you'll notice? Or pay attention to how high the bowls are stacked when they're put away, or making sure the spot where you keep your backpack is kept clear so that you're not in a foul mood the rest of the day? Do you know how difficult it is to live with you? No, you have no idea. And yet, I do it, day after day, year after year, because I love you. Nobody else will do it, Cortez. Nobody."

# CHAPTER FOURTEEN

CORTEZ STARED AT HIS MOTHER, fearful of the old age that appeared on her face. As he watched, deep seams emerged where her smile met her cheeks and around the corners of her eyes. Her hair turned from black to streaked gray, and she stooped, the hunch on her back pushing her head forward. Her laundry list of grievances wasn't finished.

"I've had to deal with finding the one brand of shirts you like because the tag doesn't scratch your back. Staying out of the bathroom at seven in the morning because that's when you use it—as if there's something special about the time! Not having friends, or meeting new people, because I need to be home to make sure the rhythms of your day aren't interrupted. The way you live isn't natural, Cortez, and you don't even know it. Haven't you ever wondered why you don't have friends? Or have never had a girlfriend before? Why do you think I was so excited to hear about Alara? Because it's never happened!"

Cortez wanted to say something at the mention of Alara, but his mother's onslaught didn't abate. All of her specific examples were obvious methods of existing in the world, and he didn't understand how any of them could cause her grief.

"Nobody else learns to talk to people by copying what they see on television. Nobody. Oh, don't think I didn't know. It's obvious when you slip into your *roles*. You do the same thing with people you meet. Your personality holds part of every teacher you've ever had. Knowing this, I get upset with myself, thinking I'm a failure as a mother because I didn't provide you with a better model. Did I not show enough examples of how to talk to people in different scenarios? Was I supposed to go through every possible situation, unaware that you wouldn't be able to use the lessons you learned from one in the other? The worst part of all this? It doesn't even work! You're no better at talking to people than if I had thrown you into the wild. You almost got yourself killed by that pimp the other day and you had no idea. You can't be left alone at any time, inside or outside the house."

The woman's age caught up with her and she started losing steam. "Maybe it's my fault. Maybe I babied you. But at the end of the day, you don't have anywhere else to go because nobody loves you like I do. You're not like other people, and the sooner you accept that the sooner you'll learn to be happy."

Cortez watched his aged mother turn and look out the window at the end of the hall. He was torn between wanting to run away and wanting to go home, between never coming back and pretending he hadn't heard her complaints. Her example demonstrated another lesson for him, one he would use just once in his time left on earth: to save up all his grievances and let them explode in a flurry of words. His bed called out to him from beyond the door. After listening to his mother reveal her issues with him and unsure of what else to do, he reached out for the door handle to try turning it once more, willing himself to grow until he was back to full size.

The lock had aged in the same way his mother had. The decades passed by while they were in the hallway, rusting the mechanism. There was a slight resistance to Cortez's turn before the lock gave way. He opened the door and a wave of stale air washed over his face, cool in the spots where tears had moistened his skin. He walked inside and went straight to the bathroom, his steps leaving footprints in a thick layer of dust. The mirror was grimy around the edges but clean in the center, and in it he saw how much damage Remy's single blow to his face had caused. His upper lip was swollen to the size of a fat red caterpillar, his nose was bloody but straight, and his teeth were all outlined by blood from his leaking gums. The water came out brown when he first turned on the faucet but became clear after he let it run. He washed the blood from his face, rinsed his mouth, and decided against brushing his teeth. When he was finished, he stared into the mirror again, wondering how he could change himself to be worthy of Alara's love. He smeared toothpaste on the bathroom counter, wondering how on earth the mess could make him easier to tolerate. No matter how hard he tried to ignore the stain it demanded his attention, and in a rush of perceived weakness he flushed it away with water. Maybe he was his mother's burden to bear.

His mother was in the kitchen when he emerged from the bathroom. She was looking through everything in the refrigerator, the open door releasing the smell of rancid food throughout the home. The floors were streaked with thin lines of remaining dust, the particles that had escaped her first attempts at sweeping. The beans and chorizo left for Cortez on a plate were covered in mold. Every vegetable had turned into a pile of mush that needed to be scraped from the surface and thrown away. She paused what she was doing and looked at her son. "There's a lot to clean up here. Why don't you go to bed and let me take care of this."

He knew they were going to act like her tirade had never happened. It was her turn to clean until he was done being mad at her, a tendency he had picked up from her in the first place. Without another word, he went into his bedroom. Time hadn't played tricks on the space—it was just how he left it. He turned on the lamp on his nightstand and was surprised to find no dust had accumulated on the surfaces of his furniture. His bed still smelled like him, like he'd slept in it yesterday and not years before. The floor was still spotless, and the clothes hanging in his closet were pressed for the next day's church service, free from moths.

From beyond his door he heard his mother crying. Cortez grew angry at every sob. She had no right to be upset. If anything, he should be upset, and yet there he was, thinking about ways he could change himself to be more worthy of love. He fell asleep wishing he could be more normal, confused about how his routines could ever be viewed as a burden, and, most of all, embarrassed that his reliance on learning to talk to people by mimicking television characters wasn't a secret.


CORTEZ AWOKE when the first rays of daylight trickled through his bedroom window. The clean and pressed clothes in his closet were cloaked in shadow, bringing the memory of the night rushing back. It was Sunday, and if his life hadn't been turned upside down, he would have turned back over and slept until it was time to get dressed for another day of worship. Instead, he sat up, a groan emanating from his aching body, and turned to the side, placing his feet on the floor. His mother's tirade still echoed through his mind. He had never considered how much of a burden he was, and finding out how much his most inno-cent actions affected her made him second-guess the organiza-tion of his life. Including going to church. This didn't bother him as much as seeing decades pass within minutes, his mother and their home both falling victim to the phenomenon. For some reason, he had been spared. Curious if it was a dream, he got up and went into the kitchen.

His mother had cleaned every speck of dust from the counters and floors. Their mustard-yellow couch, already old when they found it, didn't look any older than before. Cortez opened the refrigerator. It was empty, bare as if it was brand new, even though the exterior still showed evidence of the years. The open door released the smell of lemons into the room. The freezer was empty as well. There was no way his mother would have thrown away everything inside unless it had been spoiled; she kept tabs on their food cost with the diligence of a tax collector. The disappearance of the food was enough proof, for Cortez, that it hadn't been a dream, and after a shrug, he went to the bathroom to relieve himself.

His face's swelling had somehow gotten worse overnight. While looking in the mirror, Cortez inspected his gums, shook his loose front teeth, and poked his nose. There was a sort of masculine pride at his battle wounds. A soft chuckle brought the pain in his side into the forefront. He turned to inspect the site of the worst pain and found a dark bruise on his right side, closer to his back, from where Remy had struck him after the initial punch in the stomach. He reached across the front of his body with his left arm and poked the spot. The pain took his breath away and made his eyes roll back in his head. When his vision came back into focus, he looked again at the bruise, seeing if he could find a spot where a rib was poking out at an unnatural angle. Nothing stood out, other than the deep discoloration.

Seeing the results of the beating from the night before reminded Cortez of his discovery that Remy wasn't faithful to Alara. The hatred's heat spread through his body. Thinking of Alara, he remembered the rose he'd taken from the garden the day before. It was a lifetime ago; for the second time that morning, Cortez sensed the decades that had passed. He rushed into his room, found the pants he'd worn, and reached a hand into the pocket to find the flower, hoping it hadn't turned to dust. Its petals were still moist when he pulled out the crushed remnants, his own grip responsible for the damage. He held it up to his nose and breathed deep. Alara's scent reached him from far away, his swollen nose not letting her get any closer. He had to warn her about Remy, to tell her about his infidelity and beg her to end the relationship. With any luck, she would realize Cortez's value and leap into his arms at the revelation, thanking him with a shower of kisses. But, if he went to church, his entire day was spoken for, leaving him no chance to save her.

Alara couldn't wait until Monday.

Cortez decided to forego church with a resolve that surprised even himself, sacrificing his own salvation for the woman he loved in the same way Jesus had sacrificed himself for his flock. Cortez placed the flower next to his lamp on the nightstand and got dressed, leaving his church clothes on the hanger, instead choosing the clothes typical throughout the week: jeans and a T-shirt. Without anything to eat available in the kitchen, he decided he would wait until lunch. His plan was to warn her, receive her mountains of praise, which would ease the pain in his side, then make it back to the church in time for the postservice lunch and search for new members. There was no way he could know that she would ruin his appetite for good, and that he would never step foot in a church again.

Cortez shut the door behind him without making a sound. He thought the mechanism was silent because of his gentle touch, but the lock had been rendered useless by the passing years. The early morning sun was beginning to illuminate the streets outside his building, and in its light he saw the evidence of the flood. Piles of debris were accumulated in front of storm drains, and clothes were hung out to dry on every available surface, from both the homeless and the night creatures who'd refused to end their nocturnal escapades and escape indoors at the rain's arrival. Some parked cars were twisted, one side jutting into the street, and some were pushed up flush against the curb. The world had just been washed, the first time Cortez could ever remember it being cleaned. He was Noah walking away from the ark for the first time alongside pairs of every type of animal.

The park had welcomed the rain. Every tree sported new buds among their green leaves, and the grass had transformed into a field of flowers. Cortez could smell the sweetness in the air despite the swelling in his nose. It wasn't anywhere close to the power of Alara. He continued through the park, the lone person in Eden, and came out the other side, ready to fight the wilderness for Eve. Since it was still early, he assumed Alara would be at home; he headed in her direction.

Alara had worked the night before, closing the store late, and declined to meet Remy at a sports bar to watch his favorite soccer team, choosing instead to go home and read until she fell asleep. When the sky opened up in the middle of the night, well after her boyfriend had vented his frustration on Cortez, she was sound asleep and never heard the thunder and lightning. Her dreams included flowers. Not flowers from a budding romance, but funeral flowers, decorating an unmarked, open grave. When Cortez was walking through the park towards her home, she was lost in her dream, a ghost witnessing the lowering of a coffin, trying to figure out who was being laid to rest and having a sneaking suspicion she was witnessing the service celebrating her own life. She turned in her sleep when she discovered her specter was the lone witness in attendance.

CORTEZ WALKED onto Alara's block with his eyes scanning the sidewalks for signs of Alara's dog-walking neighbor. He spotted the tree outside what he presumed was Alara's window from the corner of the block, seeing it had also sprouted new buds like its comrades in the park. The branches looked too thin to support his weight, and he shook his head at what he had been prepared to do in the name of love—knocking on Alara's door in the first light of morning wasn't one of them. He was worried she wouldn't understand his intentions and her alarm at his knowledge of where she lived would override the quality of his information. Cars parked on the street across from the courtyard provided cover where he could observe without being seen, and he sat down to wait for his beloved to appear.

Alara left her home an hour later. Cortez grew excited when he saw movement outside her front door, and he watched her descend the steps certain she was an angel coming down from heaven. His belief was confirmed when she emerged on the courtyard in all her splendor. She wore a flowing floral dress that bared her arms and shoulders, and her hair was down, held back from her face with a thin golden headband. Her usual fabric bag hung from her shoulder.

"The queen of angels," he whispered to himself.

Alara didn't see the pair of darkened eyes watching her from behind a car as she walked across the courtyard in front of her apartment, turned, and headed into the part of the city where she worked. She was going to brunch with her friends, a Sunday tradition they held as sacred as Cortez considered church: to be missed at the risk of one's soul.

Cortez followed her. While doing so, he wondered if he could do it as a profession, imagining himself as one of the interchangeable detectives he watched on television. His track record wasn't stellar, having been caught by Remy twice now, but some hiccups could be expected for a beginner. He decided he'd look into what it took to become a detective, since he still didn't have a job, once he sealed up the case of Alara and the cheating boyfriend.

Alara's path led Cortez to a bistro with outdoor seating. She was recognized as soon as she walked up by two women her same age, both of whom stood up and gave her a hug. Seeing her with other women made her beauty stand out even more. Cortez couldn't imagine what they had in common with the delicate flower he was enamored with, and he attributed her presence with the other girls to Christian charity. There was a playground across the street with benches that provided a clear view of their table, and Cortez sat at one of them, his hunter's eyes not missing a movement.

Three more women arrived within minutes, all arriving by themselves: the rest of their party. As soon as everyone was seated, one of the group, a brunette taller than the rest with glasses, beckoned for the waiter, who came over and handed out menus. The waiter was new and didn't know the group was there every Sunday, rain or shine, the weather affecting whether they sat inside or in the sun. Friends from high school, this was when they caught up and came back together before they went back off in the directions of their own lives.

Cortez delighted in seeing Alara in her element. It was a different side of her, a smiling, happy side. His own shadow grew heavy beside him, knowing the information Cortez possessed would ruin her day. He grew restless. Sitting near the slide on a children's playground, Cortez steeled himself to walk over to her while she was with her friends.

Alara's group didn't see the man walking from the playground to the bistro, didn't notice when he tried to turn back twice before continuing while talking to himself, didn't dream the person pacing behind Alara's back was working up the nerve to talk to one of them. They were discussing one of their former teachers who had been caught up in an infidelity scandal when, from behind Alara, Cortez adopted an unaffected air and, leaning on the fence that surrounded the seating area, said, "Fancy seeing you here!"

He had seen this exact scenario played out on a sitcom whose name he couldn't remember, when a woman crossed paths with a man according to her own scheme. He imagined it would work just as well when the roles were reversed. His plan hadn't prepared him to be ignored.

Not one of the group paid any attention to him. He repeated the phrase, but louder. "Fancy seeing you here," he said, loud enough for everyone on the block to hear, before a lump of embarrassment choked off his voice.

Everyone seated outside the bistro, not just Alara's group, turned to see who spoke. Cortez stared at Alara with a sheepish smile, waiting to see her face lighting up even further when she recognized him. Instead, the light her face emitted dimmed with confusion, and she turned back around without the identity of the strange man registering.

If Cortez hadn't been sure of his mission, positive his message was of the utmost importance, he would have turned away, found a hole, and died inside. He fought the urge to run with every ounce of willpower he possessed.

"Alara," he said. He waited for her to turn around. "Can I talk to you?"

# CHAPTER FIFTEEN

ALARA HAD no idea who the person with the misshapen face was, or how he knew her name. His eyes were aflame with passion, and his whole body trembled with the strength it took to stand. She thought it was perhaps someone she had given money to on the streets by Decant; they knew her name, and her coworkers always told her they would keep coming back for more. Still unsure, she nodded, waiting for Cortez to continue.

"I'm listening," she said.

Cortez's eyes darted to the other members of her group. Some had pity in their eyes, the lips of others were contorted in disgust, but Alara displayed nothing besides divine patience for the man she didn't recognize.

"It's a private thing," Cortez said, looking down at her feet. Her toes were painted bright red, decorations on the most delicate, beautiful feet he had ever seen. He wondered what it would be like to wash them, then grew embarrassed with the primal stirrings the thought aroused. "Can we talk over there?" he said, tilting his head towards the corner.

Alara didn't miss the man's inspection, and she pulled her most visible foot back, hiding it beneath the folds of her long dress. "You can say whatever you want in front of them," she said.

"Trust me, you want to hear this alone," he said, still looking down.

"Trust you! I don't even know you!" It was the third time Alara didn't recognize Cortez.

These words stung Cortez more than any of Remy's strikes. He raised his eyes and looked into hers, pleading with her to acknowledge they had met before, begging her to admit that their interactions weren't a product of his imagination. "We talked on the bench, about your book."

An overwhelming wave of hatred for the sad man overtook Alara when she recognized the pathetic creature standing in front of her. Still mindful of appearances, and not wanting her friends to know she had a stalker—even though this was the first time she had viewed him as such—she stood and hugged Cortez, leaving him with a firsthand experience of the smell of her hair, which was better than anything he'd experienced during his feverish rose-filled daydreams. "What happened to your face? I didn't recognize you!" she said, with the grace of a seasoned actress.

"That's part of why I need to talk to you."

"Of course, let's walk over there," she said, the ball of anger in her stomach close to unbearable. She told her friends she'd be right back.

When they were a sufficient distance from the bistro that Alara could be certain her friends wouldn't hear, she turned and chastised Cortez. "You followed me again, didn't you!" she scolded. "Trying to pretend you just happened to be in the area, like I wouldn't see right through it."

Cortez wondered if every woman in his life harbored seeds of resentment deep in their hearts and were waiting for the chance to unload their burden onto his tired ears.

"What is it you have to tell me?" she said, capping another flurry of words where she called Cortez "delusional" and "creepy."

Cortez took a deep breath. "Remy's cheating on you," he said.

"One: no, he's not. Two: he's the one who did that to your face, isn't he? Did he catch you following him around too?"

Cortez told Alara the story of the night before, leaving out his reason for following Remy in the first place. He described seeing Remy at the sports bar and his own experience turning down the two women, hoping Alara would recognize his fidelity, before telling her about Remy leaving with the blond woman.

"I followed them to the pizza place, that's where Remy got me," Cortez said. He expected to be patted on the head and told he was a good boy.

Alara made no effort to hide her annoyance. "Remy already told me about helping his friend home who had too much to drink," she said.

"His *friend* was a girl!" Cortez said. He couldn't understand why Alara didn't see things from his point of view.

"Remy's got a lot of friends. Who am I to judge whether they're a boy or a girl?"

"Cheating is a sin," Cortez said, as if this explained the fault in her logic.

"A sin? Do you think I care about what *God* thinks? Priests came over from Europe, in the name of *God*, and destroyed my ancestors' entire lives. Where is my culture? Burned, because of *God*. What did *God* do when he saw the missionaries treating the Maya like *we* were the savages? *God* doesn't exist. And if he does, he's given up on us all a long time ago. What *God* thinks about sin makes no difference to me."

Cortez stood stunned. While Alara spoke, her hair levitated, surrounded her head, and turned to snakes. Serpents in the

Garden of Eden, sent by the devil to trick Adam and Eve into tasting the forbidden fruit. They disappeared at the conclusion of her speech. Cortez realized that she had exposed him to the secret seed hidden by the fruit's flesh: that the name of God was responsible for the deaths of countless innocent lives. He couldn't believe, he wouldn't believe—and he needed to save her.

"Come to church with me," Cortez said. "Listen to what the Bible has to say."

"Were you not listening to a word I said? The Bible is the problem! Men can do whatever they want, thinking they stand behind some ancient book. You know what I believe in? Love. My Bible? Whatever book I'm reading!"

"We meet every Sunday at—"

Alara cut him off. "I don't care when you meet! You all can meet in hell for all I care. Don't follow me again, don't talk to me again, I don't want to see you at Decant again. If you do, not only will I get Remy to soften you up, I'll come back and finish the job myself." She turned away and stormed off, her dress billowing behind her, leaving a trail of smoke.

CORTEZ DIDN'T SEE his mother on Sunday. After talking with Alara, he had gone straight home, unable to stomach the thought of talking to anyone; finding more people to join his church was the last thing he wanted to do. Finding out Alara's views on God and the Church had left him deflated, exhausted, and hopeless. He had been certain she was the one who could turn his fortunes around, the catalyst that would bring his father back, and her outright rejection of his faith left him disillusioned and untethered. His bed was waiting for him when he got home, and he collapsed onto it, his silent tears wetting the pillow. The smell of the crushed rose on the nightstand wafted throughout Cortez's room, wrapping him in a constant reminder of his broken heart.

He had fallen asleep at some point in the afternoon. When he woke up hungry, he went into the kitchen, opened the refrigerator, and found a plate of food wrapped in tinfoil—leftovers from the church luncheon. His mother had come home and brought it with her. Her bedroom door was closed, and he didn't need to open it to know she was inside, disappointed he'd missed church. He ate the steak, rice, and beans cold with the television turned on for background noise. The rest of Sunday passed with Cortez staring at whatever show was playing, never changing the channel, and never registering what happened on-screen.

Cortez left Monday morning and his mother still hadn't emerged from her darkness. He wanted to give up on the charade, to stop pretending he had somewhere to be, but after missing church on Sunday he couldn't bring himself to disappoint his mother any further. Going to Decant was far from his mind. Alara's declaration against God had poisoned the well of Cortez's love, and after seeing her hair transform he was certain she was the same temptation Jesus had faced in the desert: the devil, there to test his resolve. Cortez hoped to break her spell by not seeing her anymore, but he couldn't even get close to the park without hearing temptation call out his name.

Cortez walked the streets on his side of town—passing by the school where his church was held without stopping—and found himself at a corner beneath the train tracks. After looking left and right, he sat down against a chain-link fence, with his backpack beside him, content with watching the world until it was time to go back. Everyone who passed that day assumed he was new to being homeless and didn't know the rest of his brethren came out at night. Drivers stared, walkers ignored, and dogs sniffed as they passed. Two of the five dogs were on leashes. They pulled against their owners' grip, trying to get closer even though Cortez ignored them. The other three dogs were strays. They traveled in a pack with their hair matted against their bodies, victims of neglect. Cortez wished they were feral, that they would tear him to shreds, but all three sniffed him from a distance before walking away.

His mother still hadn't emerged when Cortez got home on Monday night. There was nothing to eat, so he took some money from their shared jar and went out for a cheap hamburger. Using that little amount of money heaped more guilt onto his shoulders and he wanted to, yet again, apologize for his existence. Neither the white nor the blue pills took the feeling away. Not wanting to be around people in the restaurant, he ate the burger at home, on the couch, with the television volume as low as it could go while still being audible. When he threw away his trash and saw his mother's work uniform inside the bin, he knew this episode of darkness was unlike the rest and wouldn't be over soon.

INTENT ON MAINTAINING his routine for his mother's sake, Cortez left the house at the same time again on Tuesday morning, going to the same spot against the fence. His morning was uneventful, besides the one time he had to get up and brush off the back of his pants because a procession of red ants tried carrying him away for lunch.

A group of four teenage boys found Cortez in the afternoon. They were walking back from school when they saw him sitting alone. Their leader, a cruel boy with a sharp face and messy hair, asked Cortez what he was doing. Cortez didn't answer, staring past them and pretending they didn't exist, hoping they would reciprocate and leave him alone.

"I'm talking to you," the boy said. When Cortez didn't

answer, he turned to his friends. "I think this guy's got a problem with us."

"Maybe he just wants to be left alone," the smallest in the group said.

"Well, he doesn't have to be rude," another chimed in.

The leader of the group walked up to Cortez and pushed a knee with the toe of his shoe. "You hear me?" he said.

"Maybe he's special, like the kids in that one class."

"Or maybe he doesn't like us."

When the leader of the group picked up the backpack, Cortez lunged to grab it back. He wasn't fast enough.

"So now you see us?" the leader sneered.

Cortez got up. He was taller than any of them but lighter than all but the smallest. "Give it back," he said, his voice heavy with the weight of defeat. The disappointment he'd caused everyone he cared about weighed heavy on his heart—these demons were there to punish him for his wickedness.

"You can have it back if you can catch me," the boy said a moment before running away.

Cortez didn't think twice before beginning his pursuit. They ran beneath the train tracks before turning onto a side street. The boy's friends were behind both of them, laughing. Cortez could feel his breath running out, the lack of oxygen making his legs heavy, but he kept going until he caught up with the boy at the end of an alley. He stood tall, using every inch of his height, and reminded himself he was older than them.

"Give it back," he said.

The boy thought for a moment. Cortez took a step forward. In a flash, the boy threw the backpack into Cortez's face. The backpack was empty except for his medicine, and therefore light, so it didn't cause more damage to Cortez's still-tender upper lip and nose. It did blind him long enough for the boy to rush Cortez and push him over. When he was on the ground, the leader started kicking. One of the blows landed right where Remy's fist had bruised his side; Cortez's vision flashed white with pain.

"Get him!" the leader said.

Two of the boys joined in, the smallest staying back, and the kicking stopped when they were out of breath. The leader bent down and pulled Cortez's shoulders up until they faced each other. He spit in Cortez's face, then rubbed it in.

"Shouldn't ignore people," the leader said before walking away with his friends. The smallest boy never went with them after school again.

Cortez held himself in the fetal position for a long time after they left. He was elated; the pain in his body matched his pain inside. Every breath was another reminder of what a deplorable creature he was, and he was certain God was taking steps to restore balance in the world. At some point he ended up on his back and watched the occasional cloud rolling through the blue sky, certain the angels of heaven were looking down on him and applauding him for taking his punishment like a man.

"Are you OK?" a woman's voice called out to him from the end of the alley.

Cortez didn't respond. He hoped she was there to inflict more pain on him for his sins.

The clicking of heels on pavement rang through the alley, growing closer to Cortez with each step. The approach ripped Cortez in half, his body screaming out to defend himself while his mind craved fresh punishment. His mind won, and he stayed still until the woman was right next to him. To his disappointment, she didn't strike another blow.

"Hey, aren't you the Bible kid?" the woman said.

Cortez looked into her face, crowned by the sky beyond. It was the sex worker who had taken him to her colleagues, the one his mother didn't believe God would want. "God doesn't want me anymore," he said.

The woman grabbed Cortez's arms and forced him to stand up. She brushed off his shoulders and face before inspecting the bruises on his arms. "Someone got you good, huh?" she said. "Were you trying to convince them to come to church with you too?" she said with a chuckle.

Her amusement disappeared when Cortez didn't laugh. "I was trying to get my backpack back."

"Well, you got it," she said. She looked at his face. "You're all skin and bones. When's the last time you ate?"

"Yesterday."

"It's four in the afternoon! Come on, let's get you something to eat."

She led him to a takeout Chinese spot with a window facing the street. There was no interior space available for patrons. She frequented the establishment, and knew the owner, and as soon as she approached the window he asked her if she wanted the usual.

"Make it two," she said, holding up two fingers.

The old man on the other side of the window looked confused when he saw her paying for Cortez. "You're paying for him? Now I've seen it all!" he joked.

"Shut up, Renzo," the woman replied with a smile.

She forced Cortez to eat, watching him finish every bite. "Now, what is this you were saying about God not wanting you anymore?"

"I don't want to talk about it."

"Then don't. Just listen. Look, it takes balls to walk up to a group of strangers and try to help them. You know you're the only one who's ever tried to talk to me about God? Most men are looking for a good time," she said with a chuckle.

She waited for Cortez to respond. When he didn't, she

140

continued.

"That kind of faith, it's not common. You have to hold on to it. Keep believing, even when things aren't going your way. I'd kill to believe in something the way you did when I saw you holding up your Bible to Bill. Did you know he still talks about it? He says, 'That kid had some balls.' Bill doesn't say that about just anyone, you know."

Cortez looked at her and saw her with fresh eyes. Past the makeup, past the hairstyle and choice of clothes, he saw a young woman who had a mischievous need to know what secrets the world possessed, and she was doing the best she could to support herself while she searched for answers to her unknown questions. She was beautiful, not in a sexual way, but in the way that emerges when someone knows who they are and has made peace with their existence on the planet.

The woman didn't withdraw or become embarrassed when she realized she was being seen. "Feeling better?" she asked.

"Yes," Cortez said. He smiled: not forced, not rehearsed, and not prompted by the suggestions and expectations of people who tried to impose upon him a way to exist.

"Good. Don't let your faith go to waste," she said. "And that includes wasting your time trying to get me and my friends to join your church!"

They both laughed before she tapped his thigh twice, got up, and walked away. Cortez watched until she turned the corner then began walking home, feeling better about his momentary lapse of faith but still smarting from the beating inflicted on him by the teenagers. Each breath stabbed his side, and every step exposed pain in a new joint, but the pains of his body didn't touch his mind, which viewed the world around him with a newfound certainty of purpose. His destiny was to save the Church—his mother had told him as much—and there was still time for him to figure out the best way to do it.

# CHAPTER SIXTEEN

Cᴏʀᴛᴇᴢ ᴋɴᴇᴡ something was wrong when he got home. The emptiness of the apartment was as loud as if it was crowded with visitors. It was Tuesday night, and even if his mother hadn't lost her job and had gone to work, she should be home by then. She wasn't supposed to be at church again until the following night, and she didn't go anywhere else. He opened her door and peeked in. During his walk home he had imagined he'd be opening the door to apologize. Cortez flicked on the light and saw she hadn't cleaned the decades of dust from her own room. There were lines in the dust on her empty bed's comforter and where her dirty clothes, thrown into the corner, had forced the dust into concentric circles. A thin pair of lines ran through numerous footsteps in the dust, some made by small bare feet, others by large boots. He closed the door, careful not to disturb the dust with the generated wind, leaving her room in the exact same condition as when she left.

With a full stomach, and with his mother missing, Cortez didn't know what to do. He should call someone but didn't know who to turn to for help. The former priest's number was written on a piece of paper in the drawer, a remnant from when his mother had needed to call him every night of the week during a crisis of faith a few years ago. But he was no longer their priest, transported to another country to serve a higher calling, and Cortez didn't have the number of the senior member who'd taken over the duty of shepherding for their flock. Cortez didn't know his mother kept the church directory, containing every number he could need, next to their dishes—she used it as a tray to transport plates too hot to carry.

Cortez's thoughts about who to call directed his gaze to the phone. There was a red flashing "1" on the device's tiny screen. His home never got messages because nobody ever called them. Cortez pushed play.

"Hey, Cort, how have you been? Look, I know it's been a few weeks, and you probably have another job by now, but I wanted to reach out in case there was any way you were interested in your old job. Turns out your friend Simeon is a thief. When we caught him, he told us all about how the drug deal was his idea, and he begged us to give you your job back. I think he felt guilty. At any rate, we'd love to have you back. Feel free to give me a call tomorrow or just show up; we'll hold it for you until Friday. Take care."

Cortez was left with the feeling that Simeon had another trick up his sleeve. He wanted to know why Simeon had chosen to tell the truth, and he didn't believe it was from guilt alone. Even though he sensed a trap, he allowed himself to have hope for the future; his faith was beginning to creep back and he had a job again, one that would allow him to support his mother now that she'd lost hers. He began dancing in the living room to the music in his head, and everyone looking into his apartment's window was sure the skeleton they saw dancing was death itself.

The movement and excitement shook the contents of his stomach, and the greasy food ran through his digestive tract, lubricated by copious amounts of low-quality oil. Cortez's eyes opened wide when the awareness of his body's needs became too much for him to ignore, and he ran into the bathroom, sitting down a moment before the eruption.

The phone started ringing; Cortez assumed it was his old boss once more. He tried to get up and answer but was forced to sit back down when another wave of nausea struck. The ringing stopped and the answering machine clicked on.

"You've reached the Vuscars. Please leave a message," his mother said, her voice recorded years ago.

Hearing those words from the bathroom without difficulty made Cortez's stomach drop—he would've sat down if he wasn't already seated. The number of messages displayed by the answering machine had been blinking, so he assumed nobody had heard the message from his boss. Now he had no doubt his mother could hear the answering machine from her room and had heard the message as it was being left.

"Hello, this message is for Cortez. This is the head nurse at Mercy General calling on behalf of your mother. She's in the cardiac unit, room four-eleven. Goodbye."

The answering machine clicked off.

When Cortez finished in the bathroom, he ran to the machine and listened to the message he had already heard. He repeated it twice more, feeling worse about his failure as a son each time. He convinced himself that his mother, after hearing the message left by his boss from inside her bedroom, had suffered a heart attack, and now she was in the hospital. He imagined, and was correct, that she had been lying under the blankets in her room, surrounded by darkness, too weak and exhausted from carrying the weight of the world to even get up and answer the phone when it started ringing. She had let the phone's noise pollute the apartment, hoping whoever it was would leave her alone, and had grown annoyed that they stayed on the line until the answering machine was called into action.

She hadn't recognized the boss's voice at first, but it hadn't taken her long to understand her son had lost his job, that he had hidden it from her, and that the new woman in his life, Alara, was to blame. Her heart had beaten her eyes in a race to bursting; she had found enough strength to call an ambulance before passing out.

Every decision Cortez had made over the past week replayed in his head, all of which had led to his mother's broken heart: pretending to go to the factory, not being by his mother's side at church, and obsessing over Alara. He cursed himself for eating lunch with a sex worker while his mother lay in bed because of his poor behavior in the first place.

Cortez went into his room and grabbed his Bible from the dresser. He knelt on the ground, resting his elbows on his bed, and prayed. Prayers for his mother, asking him to heal her, and prayers for the woman who had bought him lunch, that she would recognize the wickedness of her ways, change, and one day see the Lord's light. He prayed for Simeon, asking that he be punished for lying and costing Cortez his job. As soon as he uttered the words, he was struck by a twinge of uncertainty: he would never have met Alara if he hadn't been fired.

He crushed his reservations as if they were a spider creeping towards him on the floor.

"And I pray that you make sure Alara is never, ever happy for what she said about you." He didn't say, but God knew, that he wanted to make sure she was as miserable as he was about his rejection.

"Amen."

Cortez put his Bible into his backpack then opened the door to his mother's room, checking for anything she might need. Finding nothing, he left for the hospital. It was the last time he ever looked inside her space.

·  ·  ·

"IT'S ALL MY FAULT," Cortez repeated to himself as he walked to the hospital. He couldn't shake the mantra from his head, a reminder of his guilt for being the cause of his mother's inevitable last breath. To him, hospitals meant death. The institution had the same connotation for him that others reserved for "hospice," a word Cortez didn't possess in his lexicon. He had been in a hospital once before, a visit to a former member of his church who had late-stage cancer. The patient, Mr. Eckles, had been one of the few men who paid attention to the timid shadow clinging to his mother before and after the service. He was a white-haired black man in his late seventies who had relied on God's grace to preserve him from major illnesses until his sudden diagnosis and subsequent decline. Cortez's mother had dragged him to visit the man on his deathbed, drilling into his head that it was the right thing to do, disregarding Cortez's lack of resistance to the excursion. Since Mr. Eckles was a widower, the church had created a schedule so not a day would pass when he didn't have a visitor. They never said he was dying; they referred to his ultimate fate as "going home." Cortez's mother had chosen a time when nobody else from the church would be there, knowing her son's muteness would resurface if it wasn't just the three of them.

Cortez had first opened up to Mr. Eckles when he was a young boy. After Cortez's mother shared that her son was interested in joining a soccer team, and mentioned the challenges of finding a coach considerate of his lack of athletic ability—taking care to call it his temperament—the wrinkled man looked around for a piece of paper, settled on a church pamphlet, got down on one knee, and asked for an autograph.

"Sign your name so I can say I knew you before you were famous," he said with a smile, pulling a pen out of his shirt pocket and holding it at arm's length.

Cortez looked at his mother. A thin-lipped smile emerged

on her face, and she nodded. Cortez took the pen and wrote his name in big block letters, in the best handwriting he could manage. The old man brought up the signature when they saw each other at church every week, year after year, along with the question, "How's the dream going?" Cortez never had the heart to tell him that the first practice had been a complete disaster and he'd vowed to never go back, and his mother always covered for him by saying they were looking for the right situation.

Mr. Eckles hadn't mentioned the autograph when Cortez visited him in the hospital. He hadn't mentioned anything, because he didn't talk. Cortez remembered the clear plastic tube running down his old throat, the two tubes plugging his aged nose, and his own confusion about how the man was able to breathe.

"His lungs need help," Cortez's mother had told him.

The patient managed a weak smile and nod.

Cortez's mother had brought her Bible. After informing Mr. Eckles about their lives, which didn't take long, since each week was the same as the one before, she began reading various passages from the holy document. Upon completion of her selected verses, and with nothing else to talk about, she opened to random pages, reading aloud whichever passages she turned to, believing their selection was inspired by the Lord. Her fears about Cortez's silence were prescient: without the old man's urging, Cortez had nothing to say, other than "hello" when they arrived and "goodbye" when they left.

Mr. Eckles died soon after their visit. Cortez's mother sat him down and broke the news of the death with rehearsed lines meant to spare her son from pain. Cortez didn't feel anything. To him, the news of the death was like a canceled television show that wouldn't return, one enjoyable enough to watch when it was on but not addictive enough to miss. He remembered his mother's tears and, thinking about how many other people there were in the world, wondered why she was struck by the loss of a single one.

Now that his own mother was in the hospital, he understood.

THE HOSPITAL WAS over an hour's walk from Cortez's home, a trip taken with the stoicism of a flagellant, blame his implement of choice. The facility was the kind of place that never slept; those responsible for its design went to great lengths to remove the building from the surrounding city's timeline. Bright lights on tall towers lit up the asphalt moat, illuminating every parking space, the lone shadows in existence beneath parked cars. Enormous angled lights on the ground and at various heights on the building banished all darkness from the building's face. The light leaked into the rooms and polluted the night, making sleep impossible for the doctors and nurses who worked too many hours on too little rest; the impact on the health of their patients, in particular the prolonged duration of their stay due to lack of sleep, was never investigated.

A screaming ambulance screeched to a halt behind another as Cortez walked across the brightened parking lot—there was no respite from people requiring medical attention. The doors swung open and the patient was rolled in, passing by two men returning to the first ambulance with their empty gurney. The first ambulance pulled away and passed Cortez on its way back into the wild, two ragged men out to retrieve more people in need, the driver talking into a handheld device while the passenger rested his eyes.

Two pairs of automatic doors opened for Cortez as he approached. He walked into the well-lit lobby and headed straight for the front desk, proclaiming that his mother was inside. After giving the receptionist the relevant information, he was directed to a set of elevators down the hall. Taking one to the fourth floor, he then found the correct room. He peeked inside the same way he would have if he was entering her space in their shared apartment: slow, cautious, and afraid of disturbing his mother.

His mother didn't hear him come inside. She was alone, despite the presence of a second bed, staring out the window at the dark sky beyond the hospital grounds. Cortez had never seen her in such a pitiful state, and she wore her age without realizing the results of the passing years; it was the first time he saw what she looked like when she went through periods of darkness hidden in her room. Her hair was in a tangle, her cheeks were sunken, and her shoulders sagged as if she had never sat up straight a day in her life. "It's all your fault," Cortez thought to himself.

Cortez absorbed her appearance before he spoke. "Hi, Mom," he said, cautious about how he proceeded. He didn't know if she was still upset at him for missing church, if she was mad because he hadn't told her about losing his job, or if she was embarrassed her retreat into her room had caused her to lose her own.

His mother turned to him, registered his presence, then said, "Hello," letting the word linger in the air.

Cortez didn't know what to do. With her, there was always a clear path forward, a way she expected him to act and a role for him to step into. Her lack of direction meant Cortez was adrift in a sea of possibilities about what to do next, what to say, and where to go. The uncertainty was unwelcome. "How are you?" he said.

"The doctor tells me it's my heart," she replied. "I'll have to be here for a few days."

Cortez looked down and waited for her to divulge that he was the reason her heart was broken.

His mother sighed. "Sit down, Cortez," she said, pointing to a lounge chair by the window. It was beneath a tiny television, the screen black, the layout designed so patients and visitors couldn't watch together.

"You'll have to feed yourself, of course. Though you've got no problem figuring things out for yourself nowadays," his mother said with a sigh.

Cortez nodded, accepting the veiled swipe with decades of practice.

"Don't even need God now," she added.

"I'm sorry I missed church. I had to go—" He cut himself off.

"Where'd you have to go?" his mother said with scorn, her words sharp.

"I had to tell Alara her boyfriend is cheating on her," Cortez said. Confessing removed the weight from his chest. He took a big breath and waited for the attack's continuation.

"A woman keeps you away from church and you're worried about *her*? What about your soul? Or mine! Throwing me away like yesterday's garbage."

"I'm not throwing you away," Cortez whispered.

"Sure seems like it." His mother looked out the window again, letting the silence settle between them like mud to the bottom of murky water.

After she was convinced her son had suffered her silence long enough, she looked back at him and asked about the message left by his former boss. "Why didn't you tell me you lost your job?"

Cortez was prepared. "I didn't want you to worry. I thought I could get another one before you found out."

"Where did you look?"

"Nowhere," Cortez admitted. He didn't elaborate, not wanting to disclose that his new occupation was unpaid and involved following around two people on the other side of the park. It struck him that all he had done since losing his job was spend money on unneeded beverages and acquire a range of bruises, scrapes, and cuts.

"Of course not. I got you the ice cream job, remember?" she said. She had asked around at church if anyone knew of any low-skill jobs, and a member of the congregation had put her in touch with his brother, the boss at the ice cream factory. She had called the contact herself, begged him to give her son an interview, and coached Cortez on what to say.

"I thought that if I could find another job, I could make Dad proud and he'd come back for you. For us," Cortez said. He viewed every action, past and present, through the lens of his own inadequacy in causing his father's absence, and he forgot he hadn't told her about losing his job because she was lost inside her room when he got home and hadn't emerged before he left the following day.

His mother sighed. "He's not coming back, Cortez."

Cortez shook his head, not believing his mother's words. "He will, once we get ourselves settled. You said so yourself!"

"Your father only cares about one thing: the Church. He's obsessed with finding new members, bringing more people into the fold."

"And once we show how we grew our own church, he'll come back!"

"He's not coming back!" she said, her statement followed by a fit of coughing. She continued when she calmed down. "He's not coming back because I'm the one who left."

## CHAPTER SEVENTEEN

CORTEZ WAS STUNNED. Everything he thought he knew was turned on its head, and his tenuous grip on reality was slipping away. A dull ache began at his brain stem, and its tentacles spread over the back of his skull.

"You're old enough to know the truth," she said. She took a deep breath and allowed herself a long exhale before she continued. "I met your father when he saved me from a religious ceremony. He was in town to spread the Gospel and grow the area's first Catholic church. None of us had ever heard his kind of message before, talking about how we were all equal before God. Some rejected it, others embraced it, and a few listened one day then forgot the next. I knew from the moment I first heard him speak that I had found the reason I was put on this earth.

"Now, it's hard to call where we lived a town, or even a village. There was a centralized location for the leaders, but the people who worked the land never stayed in one area for very long. The views on women weren't progressive, to put it one way. By interrupting the religious ceremony, your father had unknowingly taken responsibility for providing for me; I was no longer welcome in my own family. He let me sleep in a small room near the church. In return, I made myself useful in any way I could. I helped with the sick, helped prepare food, and helped ready the church for Sunday service. Those were good days.

"Your father was the most driven man I'd ever met. It was like he could think of nothing else but how to spread the word of God. The native religion made him furious. I respected him, I feared him, and in time, I grew to love him. I like to think I kept my sinner's desire a secret, but it's hard to know for certain. As the years passed, we grew into a rhythm. I was a young woman before long, my head filled with questions and passion in equal measure. I was the last person he saw before going to bed, and the first person he saw when he woke up. In hindsight, I knew what I was doing, but at the time I convinced myself I was serving him and therefore serving God.

"One night he was upset over the death of three men in an accident. I walked him back to his room and went inside. That's the night you were conceived, Cortez. He left to Guatemala, saying he needed to retrieve a statue, promising to return. By the time he came back, I knew I was carrying you in my stomach. He flew into a rage when I told him, banishing me from the church and from his side. I took one last look at the town that had grown up around the church, while I was growing up inside its walls, and started walking. When I got to the ocean, a captain took one look at me and pitied me: it was obvious I was pregnant.

"Crossing the ocean was an experience I'll never forget. The captain said he had never been in, or heard of, the kind of storm we passed through. Not a single drop of rain fell while the boat was tossed around by wave after wave of foam. Balls of lightning ran along the deck like billiard balls, bumping into each other and the rails, making it impossible to stand on deck. I was in bed, my stomach aching, praying I wouldn't lose you in the ship's hold with nothing but men around. At some point in the storm I passed out, and when I woke up I was alone in the unmoving ship. We were docked in a harbor, and seemed to have been there for some time, because there was a connected walkway for people to come on board. A tourist found me in a daze without a single possession. They spoke English and I didn't, but we found someone I could talk to and they took me to the hospital, where I had you.

"The truth is, you were born here because I immigrated while I was pregnant with you. Your father kicked me out of the church, his church, and didn't want anything to do with you."

Cortez's mother buried her face in her hands and began to sob, releasing years of pent-up frustration. Since she always hid herself in her room when she cried, away from Cortez, he didn't know what to do. He took a white pill, sat back, and watched her, waiting.

"Those pills don't do anything," his mother said, her voice catching in her throat.

"What do you mean? The doctor gave them to me."

"The doctor gave you the blue pills; I gave you the white pills. They're sugar pills. I thought you'd outgrow them, but you never did."

Cortez inspected both bottles, ashamed at falling for the false medicine. "I'm sure he'll come back if I can find more people to come to church," Cortez said after a moment, putting the pills back into his backpack. "It's what he wants. We can work together."

"He's not coming back because he never left. He doesn't know where we are!" his mother said, grateful her duplicity was ignored—she had lived with the guilt for far too long. "Unless all of Christianity knows your name, he'll never hear of you. And even if he did, he'd never know you were his son."

Cortez wondered what he would have to do for everyone to know his name. He knew it was more than getting people to come to the small church that met in the bottom of a school, but that was a good place to start.

"Did you ever hear anything else about him?" Cortez asked.

"Never. I always wondered if there was another woman I didn't know about, one he loved more than me, and that was the reason he made me leave. There's nothing else I can come up with. I helped in the church, I stayed out of his way, I was a bridge between my people and him, useful whenever conflicts arose . . ."

"Another woman?" The memory of Remy's infidelity kicked open the door to Cortez's mind and walked in. "But that's a sin."

"Men have needs, Cortez. You'll learn one day, if you haven't already. Your father's vows didn't allow for us to be together, but we still found a way, didn't we? It's a moment of weakness like any other. God understands, and forgives; as long as you go to church each week and confess, your soul is safe."

"So you think he got rid of you so he could be with her?"

Cortez's mother curled her lips between her teeth and bit down to stop herself from crying. "It was just so abrupt. I don't see any other reason."

His mother's once-black hair—now gray—square jaw, and disconsolate eyes provided Cortez with a vision of Alara Chel's potential future, after discovering Remy was cheating on her with another woman. Cortez thought it was a fate no woman deserved, and now he understood the long-term damage rejection could accomplish. He made a vow to himself to save Alara from Remy and to bring her to church, not having given up on making his father proud.

"You're growing up too fast, my son," Cortez's mother said

to him. "I think that's why I got so upset when you missed church, because it feels like you're slipping away. Then when I heard you lost your job, I couldn't take it anymore. My body broke down."

"I'm sorry," Cortez said. He wished there was something to clean.

"Don't worry about making your father proud. He doesn't care about you, or us. Know that you've already made me proud, and there's nothing you can do to change that."

Cortez's mother opened her arms and used her fingers to beckon him to her side. Cortez stood up, walked over to her bed, then leaned over and gave her a hug.

"I love you, you know that?" his mother said.

"I know. I love you too."

"Now that you know about your father, don't bother trying to impress him anymore. He's not worth having you as a son."

Cortez nodded into her hair. She pushed him away, inspecting him at arm's length, then fixed where his hair stuck up at odd angles.

"It's late. Why don't you go home? You've been up long enough because of me."

"Well, I don't have work tomorrow," Cortez said, testing the waters with a joke.

A flash of anger, followed by disappointment, were illuminated by the bright outside lights. "You're right, you don't. Do you think you'll go back by the end of the week?"

"Maybe."

"And what happened with Simeon? He's your friend, right?"

"I'm not sure. I'll find out more when I go back."

Cortez was shooed out of the room by the back of his mother's hand. "We can talk more about everything when I get home," she said, assuming his world was turned upside down.

Her words didn't register. Cortez was lost in thought, wondering how he was going to save Alara from sharing his mother's fate, and the years of uncertainty about his father fueled the rage directed towards Remy. Balls of lightning trailed in his wake while he walked, leaving dark burns on the sidewalk from the hospital to his home.

REMY WOKE up at dawn on Wednesday morning with no idea Cortez was waiting for him to emerge from his building. He had checked the sunrise's projected time the night before and set his alarm to the same minute, typical practice during the week. His stretch routine, designed to eliminate the resulting soreness from the previous day's workout, took place in front of the large window that faced the building across the street. It took twenty minutes, and after he finished he was ready to face the day's challenges.

As a financial advisor at his father's firm, getting dressed and making himself presentable was a necessity. The job was his from before he went to high school. Each university year—where he studied finance—had been paid for in advance. His wardrobe had transitioned to a full assortment of button-downs, slacks, and dress shoes after graduation, outfits Cortez considered "church clothes." A suit jacket was reserved for days he met with his most important clients.

Remy's breakfast never varied, a quality Cortez would have appreciated if he knew of its existence. Two hard-boiled eggs, a bowl of oatmeal, one glass of orange juice, and one glass of water. He always ate in the same order: one bite of half an egg, one bite of oatmeal, half the orange juice after each egg, finish the oatmeal, then wash it all down with the water. Appearances were everything in his line of work, and he considered the care of his body a part of his job. This view was opposite from that of his father, who declared with pride that his large belly showed customers that he ate well, and that he could ensure they ate well too.

The television was on while he ate breakfast, and he turned to the sports channel. He watched the highlights and news from the day before, valuable talking points he used when he met with male clients, their typical sexual preferences making them immune to his charms. The women he met with never listened to what he said; their primary concern was the way he said it, and he had figured out from an early age that smiling while he talked was the key to winning them over.

Remy rinsed his dishes and put them in the dishwasher when he finished eating. He took a look around, making sure his marble countertops were clean and his floor spotless. In essence, his goal was to keep the place looking like nobody lived there and therefore ready for visitors at any time. He was proud of what he had accomplished in life, accomplishments he had been set up to achieve by a loving father and obedient mother, and he had never questioned the role privilege played in his life.

With a banana in one hand and his briefcase in the other, Remy left his apartment and took the elevator down to the ground floor. He told the worker at the front desk, one of five who rotated throughout the week, good morning, stopping to ask if she was just starting or just finishing her shift.

"Been here since midnight, I'm about to go home," the woman at the front desk said.

"Well, enjoy the day." He looked outside. "Looks like it's going to be a nice one."

"You too!" she replied.

Remy walked into the day's sunshine, appreciative of the morning's cooler temperature before the sun rose high in the sky and baked the city. He didn't see the man watching him from across the street.

•   •   •

CORTEZ HAD BEEN STARING at the entrance to Remy's building since before the sun rose. He had gotten home from the hospital late at night, thrown away his stockpile of worthless pills after staring at them for so long the instructions lost all meaning, and managed to sleep for a few hours before his eyes opened in the early morning. Nobody bothered him when he crossed the park and walked the now-familiar path to Remy's. Everyone continued ignoring him as he stood across the street from the luxury apartment building, assuming that anybody awake so early was a productive member of society. He was worried he would miss Remy leaving the building when delivery trucks parked in front of the building's entrance two separate times. His eyes darted to each side of the trucks, watching for his target. For an instant, Cortez thought one man was Remy, but when he stood up from against the wall and began following him, he realized he didn't recognize the gait. The possibility of Remy escaping through another door never occurred to him.

Remy started walking to work, thinking about the client meetings he had scheduled for the day. After an upcoming relaxed morning, he had a meeting before lunch, a lunch meeting, then two more before the completion of his day. As he got to the corner of the block, thoughts of the end of his workday trickled in, and while he waited to cross the street with the other walking commuters, his day's first thoughts of Alara appeared. They were logistical in nature, a study of whether there was time for her that night and if he could still get his workout in. He remembered his friends had asked him to play soccer and decided on a call to Alara around lunchtime to discuss the evening's plan. All of a sudden, he became aware of another's eyes on him, a specific gravitational pull that forced his gaze to the right.

Cortez stood next to him, a few paces behind. Remy tilted

his head back and closed his eyes. Dealing with Cortez was the last thing he wanted to do that morning. There was too much work to devote even a second to the creature who insisted on appearing in his life at the most inopportune times. He had never once feared retaliation for the beating he'd inflicted the last time they met because he didn't respect Cortez enough to think him capable of causing any real damage.

"Didn't I tell you to stop following me?" Remy said, exasperated. Confronting someone during the morning had a much different flavor than confronting someone after a night of drinking.

Cortez got straight to the point. "I have proof you're cheating on Alara." He had wondered what would come out of his mouth until the very moment the words appeared and was proud of himself for not beginning with a declaration of love for Remy's girlfriend.

"Oh you do, do you?" Remy knew he had been careful, both in his exploits and in his language with Alara, having never promised his own fidelity. It was how he could sleep at night, knowing he'd never lied to her. What she chose to believe was another matter—he knew she expected him to be faithful.

The light turned red and the signal to walk flashed on. The people who were waiting with them crossed the street, leaving the two men alone.

Cortez nodded, fearful Remy would lash out but not caring about his own well-being.

Remy had no intention of raising his heart rate before work, worried about potential perspiration. Prioritizing his occupation was a trait instilled in him by his father, and since the man was also his boss, Remy knew he was held to a higher standard. "And what about it?"

Cortez thought Remy would beg him to hand over the proof

or command him not to show it to Alara—at the very least, to pretend he cared about his relationship with the most magical human Cortez had ever encountered. The fact that Remy didn't waver in his nonchalance sent Cortez over the edge. "You're ungrateful," he said, suppressing the urge to rush Remy and tackle him to the ground.

"What can I say? I don't believe you." Remy looked at his watch, a gold timepiece his father had given him when he moved out of the house. He wasn't late. Yet.

"Oh, I have it," Cortez said. "Meet me in the library tonight and you can have it back." Getting Remy to agree to a meeting on the top floor of the library had been his plan all along.

"What is it, a picture?" Even if it was a picture, there was nothing wrong with being seen with someone. Unless Cortez had been able to snap a shot of him alone in the doorways with Liza before pizza. He was curious what the evidence consisted of, and he was also curious how he would explain away the situation to Alara if she ever got hold of what Cortez claimed to have.

"You'll have to wait and see. Tonight, top floor of the library. The light will be on in one of the rooms."

"I can't go tonight, I have a meeting I can't miss." Rescheduling meetings at a time more favorable for him was a trick he'd learned in his earliest days in the office. It was the first step in establishing power over his counterpart during negotiations.

Cortez grew annoyed at Remy's lack of appreciation at the potential loss of Alara. What could be more important than preserving her love? "Tomorrow?" he asked.

"I can be there tomorrow. What time?"

"Six," Cortez said.

Remy nodded, then turned away. By now, the light had turned back to green, and Remy had to wait for another chance to cross the street. For a moment, he feared Cortez was heading in his direction. It would lead to an awkward wait and an awkward crossing; with any luck, the thorn in his side would turn left when he turned right. His fears never came to fruition; Cortez turned around and walked away.

# CHAPTER EIGHTEEN

CORTEZ LEFT his conversation with Remy feeling like he was grateful to even get a meeting. Alara's salvation depended on them being alone, and he didn't have a plan in place if Remy declined the invitation. He walked back through the park thinking about a future with his beloved by his side, sitting between him and his mother at church because the two women in his life had become so close. Let his father stay gone, he thought, they had no room for him in their lives. If he did show up, wanting to be a part of his life after hearing about him and Alara saving the Church, he would slam the door in his face, tell him his chance was left in the prior years. Thoughts of his absent father had filled his head ever since he learned about him from his mother. Before, whenever the man was mentioned, an inflamed void opened in Cortez's heart. Now, that space had closed off, solidified, and been made impenetrable by anger.

The one thing that stuck with Cortez from his mother's confession was her suspicion about another woman. There was no pride about his lineage's responsibility for spreading the Christian message, no sympathy for the trials his mother had endured; instead, his mother's attempt to find an underlying reason why she had been tossed away haunted her son. The mother's story was Alara's story, a relationship with a man who didn't deem her special enough to swear off others. Anger at Remy had been with Cortez from the moment he left the hospital, and he'd woken up with the certainty that his prayers had been answered, that his dreams revealed what he had to do.

In the dream, Cortez had been seated on a wooden platform looking down at a fire. Brown-skinned bodies hung off to one side, tied by their hands, with their heads limp against their chests. He knew they were nonbelievers. Sinners. All around the growing fire stood his own men, their backs to the blaze, armed with thick wooden bats. They wore dirty brown priests's robes and were protecting the fire from more brown-skinned nonbelievers who stood watching the fire in horror. Anguished cries rang out from the witnesses, tears streaming down their faces. A sense of pride grew in dream Cortez as he watched the fire burn, certain the sinners would go to church after the flames of their passion died down, their introduction to the faith leading him to prominence. Maybe, if he was lucky, he had saved enough souls to convince his father to come back and welcome him with open arms, a welcome Cortez would reject, making his revenge complete.

WHEN CORTEZ AWOKE, he knew the library would have to burn before the people of the city would come to church. His father would hear about the swelling of their ranks, try to come back into his life, then be shunned for what he did to his mother. It all made perfect sense in Cortez's head, and Remy agreeing to meet him on the top floor of the library was the piece of the puzzle that would guarantee Alara was one of the people whose souls he was responsible for saving.

Back at home, Cortez sat down on the couch, waiting for the

day to pass. He had nothing to do, nowhere to go, and didn't want to see Alara again until after Remy was out of the picture. His mother was still in the hospital. Being alone as an adult for the first time he could remember offered numerous possibilities, but he didn't change a single thing, pretending instead it was a Saturday morning and his mother was still in bed—a Saturday morning that would last all day.

Cortez watched mindless daytime television: first a game show, then a talk show, then he stumbled upon a show about a small claims court, which he ended up watching for multiple episodes. When he grew hungry he ate spoonfuls of peanut butter, one of the few items in his house that hadn't expired during the weekend's storm. The setting sun cast long shadows into his apartment, throwing reflections onto the screen overtop the plaintiff. When the distraction could no longer be ignored, Cortez stood up and closed the blinds. A knock on the door at the same time made him jump.

Nobody was visible through the front door's peephole. Cortez looked left, then right, before a second round of knocking began. Confused, he looked down and saw Simeon, sitting in his wheelchair, his fist pounding on the door. Cortez unlocked the door and opened it enough to look his former friend in the face.

"What do you want?" Cortez said, trying his best to sound angry. It didn't work, and his words came out giving the impression he was constipated.

"I heard your mother's in the hospital and I came by to visit," Simeon answered.

Cortez inspected his slimy eyes and lying tongue, not trusting him for a second.

"And to say I'm sorry. Can I come in?"

Setting boundaries wasn't a part of Cortez's skill set. He frowned, nodded, then opened the door wide. He walked away, letting Simeon roll in and leaving him to close the door himself.

"How did you get up here?" Cortez said as he retook his position on the couch. He took the stairs every day and couldn't imagine how Simeon had navigated seven flights.

"The elevator. Smells terrible in there," Simeon said. He rolled next to the couch and looked at the television. Cortez turned down the volume.

"Right, the elevator. That's why I don't take it."

"No choice for me," Simeon said, tapping one wheel with his hand.

A moment of silence passed, both trying to come up with something to say.

"Your mom called the boss from the hospital," Simeon began. "She said you would come back by the end of the week, but that you'd be dealing with some extra stress."

"He left a message on the machine," Cortez said, pointing to the telephone mounted on the wall. "He said you don't work there anymore though, so how'd you find out about my mom?"

"Well, I called earlier today to see if there was anything I could do to get my job back. There isn't. But, the boss said since we were friends before, I might like to know your mom was in the hospital, in case I wanted to send a card. I just decided to show up to your building. The mailboxes downstairs told me your room number."

"You should've just sent a card," Cortez said. He looked at the muted television.

"I'm sorry, I didn't know how all this would turn out."

"Well, it's all your fault. If I hadn't lost my job, she wouldn't be in the hospital in the first place!"

"How is it my fault? I got fired too, remember?"

"Her heart couldn't handle finding out I lost my job. *That's* why she's in the hospital. And why did I lose my job? Because of you. Because you had to sell drugs."

"I was just trying to get some extra cash, for both of us!" Simeon said, raising his voice. Then, he deflated. "They caught me taking pints to sell for cash, that's why they fired me."

"That's fair. Unlike mine, where they fired me because you lied about me."

"You shouldn't have left me behind for the cops!"

"Well, you shouldn't have said anything to the boss in the first place for your own idea!" Cortez stood up, looking down at his former friend. After a moment, he said, "You should leave." It was the first time he'd ever kicked someone out of his home, and the first time he'd had to; before then, the apartment had never had visitors.

Simeon turned himself around then rolled to the door. The door opened inward, and Cortez watched Simeon struggle to navigate the confined space while pulling the door open, one hand on the doorknob and one on his wheel. A malicious joy grew in Cortez's heart, the delight of revenge. Simeon turned around after he managed to cross the apartment's threshold.

"One more thing," Simeon said, holding up a finger to Cortez from the hallway.

"What."

"Can you put in a good word with the boss for me?"

Cortez's hand took control of the situation, taking the initiative to lash out and strike Simeon in the nose. A second punch glanced off Simeon's face because, by then, his seat was already tilting back. Simeon's head hit the wall behind him, but the blow didn't knock him out. He propped himself up with his elbows and crawled forward, pulling himself away from his overturned wheelchair. A swift kick to the gut took his breath away, and he curled up into the fetal position.

"There's something wrong with you," Cortez said, looking

down at Simeon. His hands were on the wall opposite his front door, supporting his body for when his leg decided Simeon deserved another strike.

"I could say the same to you," Simeon sputtered. In response, Cortez stomped Simeon's flaccid knees with his right foot. Simeon laughed, knowing his legs hadn't registered a sensation since the day he was born.

One of Cortez's neighbors, a middle-aged man with thick glasses and a mustache, poked his head out and asked if everything was alright. Cortez took one look at him with a maniacal look in his eyes and he shut the door.

"What's so funny?" Cortez demanded.

"My legs are already useless," Simeon responded with a pained chuckle.

Mrs. Wyatt, who lived on the opposite side of the hallway from the middle-aged man, emerged from her apartment. Her youngest child, shirtless but wearing a diaper and turquoise socks, stumbled out and held onto her leg. "What are you doing, young man!" she screamed, beginning to rush forward.

Cortez turned to her. Something in his gaze stopped her in her tracks. "Mind your own business," he said. He looked down at Simeon and got a sense of being Remy, looking down on a weaker victim with disgust.

"Don't let me see you again," Cortez said, doing his best to say the words the way he imagined Remy would say them. He turned around and went back into his apartment, slamming the door behind him. Watching through the peephole, he saw Mrs. Wyatt right Simeon's wheelchair and help him into the seat. While she brushed off his shoulders, Simeon looked right at the peephole and smiled.

No matter how hard she tried, Cortez's mother could never scrub away the shadow that Simeon saw in the space between the bottom of the door and the floor.

. . .

THE NEXT DAY, Cortez got to the library early in the afternoon. The sun was still high in the sky, and the people enjoying the weather, the ones whose jobs didn't tie them to a desk from nine to five each day, partook in a collective laugh at the expense of those who lived and died by the clock. He stood in the park, watching the flow of people he didn't care for going in and out of the entrance, past the pillars and through the massive wooden front door. The enormity of the wide steps in front of the library overwhelmed him. The proximity of the books to the trees, whose sacrificed cousins contained millions of knowledge's words, created dozens of leafy witnesses who stared at Cortez as if they saw the flames in his heart. He couldn't ignore their gaze, and, to settle his soul, even if for a moment, he walked around the building and entered through the rear door.

Compared with seeing the entire library bustling with children during his last visit, the rear entryway was suffused with loneliness. The few people present were silent, their steps muted, as they walked through the smaller lobby. A person at the desk asked for his library card when he approached.

"Nobody asked for my card last time I was here," he remarked as he handed over his card.

The young man at the desk assumed the statement was a complaint. "They should have," he said while he scanned the card.

"There were a lot of kids here," Cortez added.

"Oh, you came during the festival," the library worker said, his attitude changing. "It's a nightmare trying to get everyone to scan then." He handed Cortez's card back to him. "But, according to the rules, we still should've."

Cortez took the card and continued past the desk. He passed a man and woman walking out, each with a book in their hands, keeping his eyes down so he didn't have to acknowledge their presence. In his pocket, bulging against his leg, was a can of soup. It was the heaviest thing he could find in his house, and he hoped it was enough to get the job done. The lighter his mother kept for birthday candles was in his other leg's pocket.

He found the librarian's stand on the second floor of the library, abandoned. He milled about, waiting for someone who could help him. A book about military helicopters on the counter caught his eye. He picked it up, began turning through its pages, and was pleased at the numerous pictures. The time-line of helicopter technology ran from early drawings by Da Vinci about the theoretical machine to modern sand-colored war helicopters. The librarian arrived as he was skimming through the various weapon systems.

"Can I help you?" the librarian asked. It was the woman with green glasses who always wore a shawl.

Cortez remembered the woman's name: Gertrude. He wished he knew the name of the other librarian, the nice one, the one who had helped him despite Gertrude's reluctance. He thought she'd be a good woman for him, if he wasn't sold on Alara.

"I need to check out a book. *Love in the Time of Cholera,*" he said, smiling while putting the book about helicopters back down on the counter.

Cortez's cheap impression of a smile stirred something in Gertrude's memory, and she remembered their interaction the weekend before. It had been a busy day, so busy she'd almost forgotten the man who took the warmth from the room. She got goosebumps when she recognized him, shaking her head as she wrapped her shawl tighter around her shoulders. She had never associated Cortez's presence with the temperature change since she lived in a state of perpetual cold.

"I helped you find that a few days ago," she said. She looked beneath the counter. "Elisabeth still hasn't put it back," she said, annoyed.

"Thanks," Cortez said, staring at the cover.

"Did you need anything else?" Gertrude asked.

"Yes, I'd like to watch a movie on the top floor," he said, holding the book by his side.

"Those rooms are for educational purposes only," Gertrude replied.

"I've done it before," Cortez said.

"What did you want to watch?" Gertrude acquiesced with a sigh, wanting to rid herself of the visitor. She would have made Elisabeth handle the man and the problem her charity had created if the woman had been working that day. As it was, she cursed her coworker for showing Cortez sympathy in the first place.

"I don't care," he said. He traced the helicopter on the cover of the book with his index finger. "Something long."

The librarian's eyes pierced Cortez through her green spectacles. She waited for him to notice her glare, but he never looked at her face. Giving up, she told Cortez to follow her.

Together, they went to the selection of movies. Seeing his interest in the military helicopters and assuming his tastes included all facets of war, she chose a four-part documentary about World War II. "This one is long, especially if you go through all four parts," she told him, handing him the first installment.

"Can you give me all of them?" Cortez asked.

Gertrude almost said no, almost confronted him about what he was running away from that he wanted to spend hours watching television at the library, but instead nodded and handed him the discs in their plastic containers. "Hours of entertainment," she said.

Cortez didn't pick up on the sarcasm. He thanked the librarian and confirmed he could use any room on the top floor.

"Some of the rooms don't have TVs," she said. "The rooms on the other side of the stacks just have desks. You won't be able to use those."

"Stacks? I didn't see any when I was up there last time."

"Magazine stacks. They're behind the first hall of rooms. If you didn't walk very far down the aisle you wouldn't have seen the cut-through."

Cortez thought about the stacks, considered the ways he could use them. "Filled with magazines, huh?" he said, his plan coalescing.

"And bundles of newspapers. The stuff nobody uses except the journalists." Gertrude started walking back and Cortez followed. "The library saves what everyone ignores," she said with pride.

"Good to know," Cortez said. He turned into the staircase as they walked past it, leaving Alara's favorite book on a shelf near the break in the bookshelves. The librarian was left describing the various magazine and newspaper subscriptions the library had collected over the years, and the task of cataloging the numerous volumes, to the air around her. When she turned around and noticed her words were wasted on thin air, she shook her head and cursed Elisabeth once more for empowering the strange young man.

Cortez walked up the stairs and past the room where he'd watched the movie that taught him Remy had to die before he could be with Alara. He found the space between the rooms that led to the stacks that Gertrude had mentioned and, walking through, found a vast expanse of metal bookshelves. They all reached to the ceiling, each one holding a different number of magazines, depending on the width of the spine. An entire collection of thin magazines about the advancement of chemical processes was on a single shelf, while the collection of landscape architecture magazines, thick with pictures, took up all the shelves on two full bookcases.

Cortez found the newspaper bundles behind the rooms near the entrance, at the farthest point from the access point that ran through the rooms. Newspapers from every major city in the country, with small placards beneath each stack of bundles, were all tied up with twine and a neat bow on top.

After his inspection of the area behind the rooms, Cortez returned to the aisle and chose the room farthest from the staircase, turned on the light, inserted the movie, and began waiting.

# CHAPTER NINETEEN

REMY WAS STILL at work while Cortez was in the library. He had scheduled meetings all day, and not once did he give any consideration to his day's final meeting, the one with Cortez. After Cortez's initial confrontation, when he'd learned evidence of his cheating existed and was in Cortez's possession, he decided that, regardless of the outcome, he would deny it if confronted by Alara. It was his duty, as a man, to hold his ground, not to admit his sampling of other women, in order to preserve his honor. Denial would also be helpful for her, would give her peace of mind, and the last thing she needed was to second-guess her own quality as a woman because Remy wanted to taste other flavors. His day had started the same way every other day began, and his meetings ran like clockwork, efficient chunks of time where he could say anything and still collect money. He told his father about his success after each meeting, where prospects transformed into clients; the man then congratulated him, told him how proud he was of him, and urged him to keep up the momentum.

When Remy looked at his calendar and saw he had no more work meetings that day, he tilted his head back and succumbed to the dread of meeting Cortez. He was annoyed the man was taking his time, his most precious asset, and he had to tell Alara he couldn't pick her up from work before dinner; their date had been planned before Cortez approached him on the street, and he had forgotten about it when he agreed to the time. When he left the office at quarter to six, the secretary told him to have a good night.

"We'll see about that," he said, letting the pronouncement hang in the air.

Remy didn't know the library's location because he'd never been there before; his father had bought any books he needed for school brand new. He looked up his destination's address before he left the office and was surprised the institution was in prime real estate, next to the park in the heart of the city. His surprise doubled when he approached the imposing stone building, with its wide staircase and extravagant carvings atop broad pillars, and he wondered why he had never been there before. For the first time in his life, he experienced a twinge of regret for never having visited the library as a child, and for not reading any books as an adult. The grandeur of the design betrayed its power, and Remy vowed to return under different circumstances to investigate what the city's planners deemed important enough to devote such vast resources to keeping safe.

After walking up the front steps and feeling his legs burn, he looked around and wondered why nobody was using them for exercise. His head was filled with the ways he would train in the space when he pushed open the immense wooden doors and entered a lobby that rivaled any in the city.

"Hello," the women at the front desk said in unison. Both had on glasses, wore their hair tied back, and had on no makeup —the type of women Remy expected would be drawn to work in a place full of books.

Remy nodded and kept walking, intent on getting his meeting over with as soon as possible.

"You have to scan your card," the woman closest to him said, her cheeks flushed.

"Card?"

"Your library card. We can issue you one if you don't have one."

This was how Remy got his first library card. He used it once.

Remy left the women behind, giggling, telling them he'd be back to say goodbye before he left. He went in search of the way to the meeting's location. Climbing the main staircase in the lobby brought him to the second floor. Once there, he approached the librarian and asked about getting to the top floor.

Gertrude shook her head, annoyed that, for the second time that day, a young man had requested access to the area that was reserved for educational purposes. But one look into Remy's eyes erased her reluctance and spread tentacles of warmth throughout her body. "The staircase is back there," she said, pointing to where Cortez had disappeared and left her talking to herself. "What do you need help with?"

"I'm meeting someone up there," he said, scowling.

Remy turned away and left Gertrude wondering what kind of arrangement the two very different young men had that required them to watch a long movie. She reminded herself that love takes many forms. She got the urge to check on them if they didn't come down soon, then decided against it because she didn't want to walk in on them in an embarrassing situation. She assumed the charming young man's smile hid his secret, and if he didn't need her help with books, she could at least provide a measure of privacy.

. . .

THE ONLY ILLUMINATED room on the fourth floor was at the far end of the hallway. Remy shook his head, frustrated at Cortez for making his life difficult and not choosing the first room. The walking wasn't what bothered him, it was the extra time; he wanted the confrontation finished. A sliver of trepidation entered his mind while he walked through the unlit darkness, wondering what kind of proof Cortez could have. Why had Alara ever brought the pitiful creature into their lives in the first place? He toyed around with the idea of letting Cortez give her the evidence and inflict pain on her heart, as punishment for giving a parasite access to their lives. Lost in thought, Remy didn't notice the space between the rooms that led to the magazine stacks and bundles of newspapers, or the eyes peering at him through the darkness.

Remy stood outside the closed door. The blinds were drawn closed. From seeing inside the other empty rooms, he knew the enclosed space was small. He snorted and shook his head, thinking about Cortez's foolishness—the man was no match for him and posed zero physical threat.

Cortez watched Remy stand in front of the closed door from the aisle that cut through to the stacks. He'd never imagined his target would stand still for so long. It was as if he was waiting for Cortez to sneak up behind him and attack. The moment before Cortez made his move, Remy reached forward and walked into the study room, leaving Cortez alone in the dark hall.

Opening the door released the sound of the playing documentary into the top floor. The narrator was talking about German propaganda efforts leading up to and during the Jewish population's internment. The room was empty, and Remy thought perhaps this was a message from Cortez. He spent the next few moments staring at the screen, wondering how his situation was similar and what Cortez implied by showing him this material. His best guess was that Cortez thought he was leading Alara on in a similar way to how the Germans led its citizens to believe their lies about the Jewish population, but he dismissed the comparison as ludicrous. As the narrator continued on about the power of words to shape the future, Remy was struck in the back of the head by a can of soup.

The way Cortez had imagined it, the blow would knock Remy out. It was how it was always done in the movies, except they used the butt of a gun. When Cortez tried to recreate the scene in real life, his victim stumbled forward, his hand on the back of his head, annoyed.

"What was that?"

Knowing it would have been safer to hit a beehive than to stay in the small room, Cortez turned and ran into the rows of magazines. He had a head start on Remy, and while he ran he looked down at the can in his hand. It was dented on the side because Cortez had held it sideways when he struck. The new dent made it easier to palm.

"What the hell's the matter with you?" Remy yelled from the aisle that cut through the rooms. He didn't know where Cortez was, but he knew he was among the shelves. He started walking forward, peering down one aisle at a time.

Cortez was on the far side of a long bookshelf, hoping his heavy breathing wouldn't give him away. Fear rose from his legs, urging him to flee, but he suppressed the feeling with the certainty that he was saving Alara. God would smile down on him as long as he did what was necessary for love. His love for her made everything manageable, the whole world—even its distasteful parts—palatable, and Remy was the one thing standing in their way. In *his* way.

When Cortez heard Remy's voice pass from his right to his left, he ran down the aisle on his right. He didn't notice Remy had stopped speaking, calling his name, or asking him questions that would never be answered. Cortez clutched the can in his hand and peeked around the corner.

Remy had guessed Cortez would try sneaking up behind him. It was just the type of thing the coward would do, catch him when his back was turned instead of facing him like a man. When he was walking forward, looking down the aisles, he was laying a trap, always certain the true threat was behind him, not ahead. Once he got close to the far wall he stopped talking, certain it was a matter of time before Cortez emerged to finish the job. Remy wouldn't let him. He snuck from bookshelf to bookshelf, slow when he turned the corner of each, ready for Cortez to emerge. He didn't have a sense of what he would do when he caught him, since hurting him with his fists hadn't produced the desired results, and he couldn't imagine any amount of pain would stop Cortez's pursuit.

Both men saw each other with an entire aisle's width between them—Cortez crouched, Remy standing tall. After a breathless moment where neither man made a move, Cortez pulled back and Remy ran after him. The chase didn't last long; although Cortez ran for his life, Remy exercised every day. Remy tackled Cortez, knocking the soup can from his hand.

Remy's firm grip held Cortez fast when the pursued tried scrambling away. Remy climbed to his knees and his first punch landed right in Cortez's stomach. All of his anger towards the interloper came out in a flurry of body strikes, leaving Cortez with a sore liver, bruised kidney, and swollen spleen. Before Remy exhausted all of his anger, he stood up and pulled Cortez to standing. "You're going to show me this evidence you have," he said, pulling Cortez by the shirt back towards the room now educating the hall's air about the German treatment of the Jewish population.

Cortez allowed Remy to drag him the length of the aisle. Through watering eyes he saw they were about to reach the end of the bookshelf and turn back towards the cut-through and the room. Thoughts of Alara, of how grateful she would be when she found out he'd saved her, trickled into his mind, replacing the pain. When Remy turned the corner, Cortez pushed with all his might, twisting away. Remy's grip never faltered; Cortez's shirt ripped. He ran back down the aisle, in the direction from where they came, and dove for the soup can.

Remy, in close pursuit, had reached out to grab a hold of Cortez the moment he dove. Reaching through thin air caused him to lose his balance and he fell. He got back onto his knees and scrambled towards Cortez when a blow struck him in the mouth. He tasted blood and discovered stones rattling in his mouth.

"My teeth," he said, his hands under his chin, catching both blood and pieces of chipped tooth.

That moment was the opportunity Cortez needed. With all his might, he wound up and smashed the edge of the soup can against Remy's skull, behind his ear, knocking him out.


REMY WOKE up with a throbbing headache, the pain radiating down to the base of his neck. He was seated with his chin down against his chest, the weight of his skull too much to bear. His eyes fluttered open then closed when they realized full exposure to the room's light was overwhelming. Unable to focus, he saw what looked like throw-up on the left side of his shirt through the blur. He took a deep breath, allowing the internal air pressure to lift his chin while keeping his eyes closed. In the background he heard about the German war strategy: blitzkrieg. Strike fast, with power, to break through the opponent's defenses. The smell of tacos reached his nostrils. Once he identified the smell, he couldn't ignore it. The vapors surrounded him, emanated from him. He didn't remember eating Mexican food. Thinking about what he ate that day jogged his memory: leaving work, going to the library, and Cortez. He opened his eyes wide, ignoring the pain, forcing them to take in the world around him as he came back from the darkness.

Seated in front of Remy, his back to the television, was Cortez. His hands were folded on the table, patient hands matching his patient face. He was waiting for Remy's return from unconsciousness with pleasure.

Remy lunged forward, and sharp bites cut into his wrists. Leaning back, he found his legs tied to the chair, each one lashed just above the ankle. He stared at Cortez, enraged.

"What did you do?" he said.

Something in Cortez had changed while Remy was unconscious. The man seated across from him was both disconnected and alert, like a puppet master watching his performance from above. His hair stuck out at odd angles, his shirt was stretched and torn; nevertheless, he exuded the tranquility of someone who had accepted their purpose in life and was committed to seeing it play out until the end. Each breath Cortez took produced a smiling grimace, the pain welcome, a reminder of his sacred duty.

"I tied you up!" Cortez said in a singsong voice, as if nothing could be more obvious. His pupil had asked a frivolous question that produced a wonderful teaching moment.

"Why?"

Cortez grinned, followed by an almost imperceptible tilt of his head and batting of his eyelashes. "So you couldn't come after me anymore! You were going crazy." Cortez held an index finger to his head, swirling it around his temple.

Remy tried to pull his hands apart. His wrists received a second biting sting for the effort. "Where did you get the rope?"

"Oh, there's *tons* of it," Cortez said in an offhand manner. "The library uses it for the newspapers."

The library. Remy thought about the librarians below, wondering if any of them had heard their skirmish. He looked at Cortez, inspected the smiling face.

"Help!" he yelled out as loud as he could. "Help! I need help!"

Cortez made no effort to silence his prisoner. He stared at Remy, delight in his eyes. "The door's shut, Remy. They can't hear you."

Yelling created an unbearable pressure behind Remy's eyes. He shut them and bowed his head, trying to calm himself with deep, even breaths. Immobilization in the chair produced a sense of helplessness he had never before experienced in his entire structured life, and he couldn't ignore the agitation in his gut the state produced. The smell of Mexican food reached his nostrils once more. He opened his eyes, looking at the remnants on his chest. There were pieces of cubed chicken, corn, and beans, all unchewed. "Did you pour soup on me?" he asked.

Cortez pulled his lips away from clenched teeth, looking sheepish. "Sorry about that," he said, standing up. He walked around the table and brushed the food from Remy's chest, then wiped his wet hand on his pant leg. "Chicken tortilla soup. I just picked a can from the house. It exploded."

Remy shook his head, unable to believe what Cortez was telling him. The ridiculousness of the confrontation made him chuckle, then laugh. "You're telling me . . . you asked me to come to the library . . . so you could knock me out with a can of *soup*?" Remy said, howling with laughter.

Cortez sat back down and laughed along with him. "That was the plan," he said. "I got lucky with the newspaper bundles."

"Lucky?" Remy said.

Cortez pulled the lighter from his pocket and flicked it, creating a small flame. "I would've had to act faster if I couldn't tie you up." A dark shadow passed over Cortez's face, making his face, with its sunken cheeks, look like a skeleton with two glittering chunks of anthracite in its eye sockets.

Remy choked on the awareness of Cortez's ultimate plan. On the television, the narrator started discussing the creation of the concentration camps.

"Why don't we forget this ever happened?" Remy said. "We can go our separate ways, put the whole thing behind us."

Cortez slammed his fist against the table. "I don't want you to forget, Remy. That's all you do, forget about everyone else but you. Like you're the only one who matters around here! You forget, Alara forgets; everyone forgets about me!" He stood up and started pacing the room, talking to Remy as if he were a member of a vast crowd of listeners who, now that he had their attention, Cortez wouldn't let go without them hearing what he had to say. "My whole life I've done the *right* thing. Done what people expected of me. And what do I get for it? Nothing! I get left behind, ignored—" He turned to Remy. "Forgotten. It's time people like you learn you aren't untouchable."

"People like me?" Remy said, lashing out with his own anger.

"People on your side of the city! You all act like we don't exist on the other side of the park. The part that needs to stay hidden—out of the limelight, away from the world. Well, I have news for you, *Remy*. We aren't all drug dealers! We aren't all insects hiding in the shadows, scurrying around at night. What if we want to see the daylight too? What if I want to be seen? Did you ever think about that?" Cortez punctuated the final word with a slap on the table.

# CHAPTER TWENTY

REMY STUCK a finger in Cortez's open wound. "You're just mad Alara doesn't want anything to do with you."

"She's never had the chance! Poisoned from living on this side of the city, from being around *you*." The words dripped from his tongue. "I'm the one who can save her, the only one." Cortez lit the lighter and stared at the flame.

"Save her? What are you saving her from, me?" Remy asked, fueled by impotent rage.

"Saving her soul! You don't deserve her." Cortez extinguished the flame then paced while he gathered his thoughts; Remy waited for him to continue. "She needs to learn about Jesus, to study God's word. She reads all those books but doesn't read the Bible. She's going to hell, Remy, unless she changes. And you don't even care."

Remy's mouth opened but no words came out. He wasn't prepared for another battle to add to the numerous wars caused by religion throughout history.

"You know she said she doesn't believe in God?" Cortez said. "She said she believes in love."

"She's told me. She blames your God for murdering her ancestors."

Cortez ignored the attack on his faith. "Believes in love but doesn't believe in Jesus's love. He loved humanity so much, he sacrificed himself to erase our sins."

"I don't think that's what she meant when she was talking about love." Remy tried to wiggle his hands, seeing if he could find any slack in the rope. By putting pressure on one hand, he could create more space for the other.

Cortez turned on Remy. "Of course that's not what she meant! Because she doesn't know any better. And I can't show her the right way if you're still around."

"So what, are you going to kill me?" Remy said, his jaw locked in defiance.

"I won't." Cortez looked down at the lighter and flicked on the flame again. "The flames will."

Remy worked the rope down his hands, gaining slivers of freedom one hand at a time. His shoulders shifted in a way that created suspicion in Cortez, who walked around to inspect the knots.

"You almost got them out," Cortez said, laughter in his voice. He tightened the knots, making the rope stab Remy's wrists. "Even if you did, your legs are still stuck."

Remy shook back and forth on the chair, alternating slamming the front and back legs in frustration. "If I get out of here—"

"You won't," Cortez said, cutting him off. He reached into Remy's pocket and took out his cell phone. He looked up Alara's name and called her before putting the phone up to his ear.

There was no answer.

Reaching into his own pocket, Cortez withdrew a slip of paper. "I wrote down the number before I came, just in case," he explained while dialing. "Hello? Hi, yes, is Alara working today? . . . She is? . . . OK, can you tell her the library is on fire? . . . It doesn't matter who this is, I just know she'd want to know." With that, he hung up and put the phone back in Remy's pocket, returned to the opposite side of the table, and sat back down. With his hands folded on the table, he looked at Remy, smiling. "Now, where were we?"

ALARA WAS MAKING a latte when her phone vibrated in her pocket. Strict company policy prohibited use of phones, citing sanitation reasons, but every barista at Decant kept theirs stashed on their person for when the line of customers receded and gave them a moment to communicate with the world outside the coffee shop. A quick vibration meant a message, continuous a phone call. Everyone who had Alara's number knew not to call her, ever, because she wouldn't answer. When her phone continued vibrating while she lidded the drink she had made and handed it to the waiting customer—this particular customer always got the same sized latte, at the same time, every day—she sensed the continued vibration's significance. With a line of drinks still to go, and a cluster of customers waiting for those drinks across the counter from her, she risked a peek, withdrawing her phone just enough to see the front screen and discover that her boyfriend was calling her.

She had been cold towards Remy ever since Cortez informed her about the other woman. Her woman's intuition, deep down, confirmed that the pitiful creature had been telling the truth, though his pained, awkward delivery rankled her to the core. She had seen Remy just once since Sunday, at dinner on Tuesday, where she listened to him go on about work problems, exercise accomplishments, and sports news, never once asking her about herself. She had mastered the art of listening long ago. Remy never suspected her shadow had turned away from him and was searching for a way out. They'd spent the night together at her place, sleep preceded by physical satisfaction that turned her thoughts away from her situation for the duration of their love, but, once he finished and gave himself over to sleep, she lay awake, wondering how many women had experienced the thrusts of his passion since they had first started dating. Remy was gone the next morning, off to work, leaving Alara alone to unravel, in the light of day, how she would untangle herself from the mess she was in.

The coffee shop's phone rang right after the vibration in her pocket stopped. The supervisor, a man who made the hairs on the back of Alara's neck stand on end, answered, looked at her, then nodded while saying, "Yes." Alara poured milk into the next drink on her docket, a mocha, topped it with whipped cream, and handed it off with a smile that disappeared as soon as she turned around and looked in the landline's direction.

The supervisor was balding despite being in his late twenties but insisted on growing what hair remained to shoulder length, tying it back in a ponytail while on the clock. His skin possessed a constant sheen, a combination of sweat and oils that had resulted in consistent acne for over a decade, with the associated scarring to match; there was too much junk food and too little physical exertion outside his time spent at work for him to outgrow the affliction. He was a tall man and wide in both directions; whenever the baristas worked with him, providing enough navigable room for him behind the counters was an added part of their job. Shifts with Alara were circled on his personal calendar, looked forward to until they arrived and relished during their execution.

Alara, on the other hand, dreaded shifts with this supervisor. She could never shake the sensation that he was staring at her, taking in the shape of her body during every trivial movement. Now, she watched him approach, knowing the phone call to Decant was for her, that Remy had called the store when she didn't answer her phone.

"The library's on fire," the supervisor said. His chapped lips were outlined by a thin red line.

The floor fell away and Alara put a hand on the counter for support.

"They didn't say who it was," he added.

Alara knew it was Remy. What she didn't know, and couldn't figure out, was how her boyfriend had knowledge of the library fire in the first place, and why he thought she should know. He hadn't shown the least interest in books as long as she'd known him, and she stopped talking about books she was reading with him long ago. Her heart warmed one degree towards Remy, a trapped woman impressed by the slightest gesture of goodwill in a frigid relationship. She leaned back and looked at the register, taking note of the time.

Forty minutes remained on her shift.

In the library, Remy knew the end was near. There was no uncertainty in the crazed man's voice, no second-guessing during the entirety of his tirade. "She'll never love you."

"You're wrong. I've already seen this story played out!" Cortez said. His childlike delight had returned in full, banishing the anger to the shadows. Anyone who entered the small room on the top floor of the library at that precise moment wouldn't have believed the man was capable of the vitriol that had spewed from his mouth moments before. Pictures of different medical experiments performed on Jewish people during the Holocaust flashed on the television.

"Where, in the *Bible*?" Remy sneered.

Cortez closed his eyes and shook his head. "No," he said with an exhale, calming himself. He opened his eyes. "You think you're *so* smart, don't you? It's actually a book Alara is reading now. Her favorite, in fact. She said so herself."

When Cortez stopped talking, Remy jutted his chin forward and raised his eyebrows, encouraging Cortez to continue.

"*Love in the Time of Cholera.* Have you ever heard of it?"

Remy shook his head no. "I don't read," he said with an outsized dose of pride.

"You should try it sometime." Even though Cortez hadn't read the book himself, watching the movie was just as effective in his view, a way to get the information much faster than reading permitted. "Anyways, in the book, the main character falls in love with a girl. Of course, right, that's why we're here in the first place!"

Cortez wanted Remy to acknowledge his assessment of the situation; he continued after a nod from the captive man.

"Well, here's where it gets good. And why it relates to us! In the story, the girl rejects the first guy, who truly loves her, and marries another man because of his money. That's you and me!"

"You don't have money," Remy said.

"No, you're the one with money. I'm the one who loves her!"

"You're the rejected one."

Cortez glowered. "Yes. The rejected guy waits years for the guy she married to die, so they can be together in their old age." Cortez looked at Remy, waiting for recognition of his quality analysis. It never came. "I figured, why wait, you know? Why not get rid of the guy so I don't have to wait all that time?"

Remy stared at Cortez. "You sat here talking about how you wanted to save Alara's soul, how you wanted her to learn about God, but really you want her for your own selfish reasons! And you're willing to kill to get her."

Cortez's eyes welled with tears when faced with his own hypocrisy. "No, that's not it at all!"

"You just said so yourself," Remy said, calm in the face of mania.

"Stop confusing me!" Cortez whimpered. He lowered his face between his elbows and joined his hands behind his head.

"Look, I'm just trying to understand," Remy said. "I'm sorry that I wrote you off, ignored you. I shouldn't have done that. You're worth more than that, and Alara would be lucky to have a guy like you."

Cortez lifted his red, tear-streaked face. "You mean that?"

"I do. I think she'd be very happy with you. Good luck getting her to church though."

The two men shared a laugh. "I think she can help me save the Church," Cortez said.

"Save the Church?" Remy knew the time for his final request was coming. The timing had to be perfect; he couldn't rush because Cortez could be scared away. His strategy was the same as catching a butterfly without a net: wait for it to land on his arm.

"Our church needs more members. I go out every week but never convince anyone to come with me," Cortez said, meek as a lamb. "If I could get Alara's help, I could save the Church."

"I'd go to church with you," Remy said. It was almost time.

Doubt crept into Cortez's mind. Misjudging Remy would turn his holy act of killing to save the Church into murder, in direct opposition of the Ten Commandments.

"We could save it together," Remy added.

Cortez was blindsided by the proposition. It was an option he'd never considered, not in his wildest dreams. In a flash of jealousy, he imagined his father hearing about Remy's exploits to save the Church, ignoring Cortez's contribution. Thinking about his father reminded him of the man's suspected infidelity, enraging Cortez and reminding him why he hated Remy in the first place. His prisoner was lying about saving the Church, the same way he'd lied in his other relationships. Remy was cheating on Alara, making a fool of her, the same way his father had done to his mother. He couldn't forget, he wouldn't forgive, and Remy's kind smile sowed suspicion in Cortez's heart.

"We won't save it together, because you won't be around to help," Cortez said with finality.

The distance Cortez traveled in the space of a few breaths made Remy scramble for a hold on a situation that was slipping away from his grasp. A moment before, Remy had been certain he was close to gaining Cortez's confidence. Now, he knew he had to take his long shot, that soon there wouldn't be another chance.

"Why don't you untie me so we can go find some souls to save?" Remy said.

Cortez laughed. "And share the glory with you? You've had your chance, and you squandered it. You had Alara and she wasn't good enough for you! You run around with other women, acting like you're untouchable. It's time for someone else to have a chance, someone who won't ruin the opportunity because they actually appreciate it!"

"Look, I don't know what else to tell you. I underestimated you and how much you care for her. Let me go and you won't see me again."

"You'll run to the police the second you leave here; I'm not dumb."

"No I won't, Cortez, we've got work to do."

Cortez stood up, paced the room, then told Remy he needed to think before leaving the room. Remy strained against the ropes on his wrists and ankles, using every ounce of strength he had accumulated during his years of training. For his efforts, he was left with four patches of torn skin and bloodless extremities.

Defeated by the knots, Remy looked at the television. The narrator was discussing the chemical properties of Zyklon B and talking about the delivery mechanism, how the masses were told they were being deloused and washed off. The victims died in twenty minutes.

CORTEZ WALKED in carrying two bundles of newspapers. He put them on the ground before turning around and leaving the room. Once Remy realized what was happening, he used each opportunity to plead with Cortez to let him go, telling his captor he could help him save the Church, that he wouldn't tell the police, and that he would let Alara go without a fight.

Any doubts Cortez had harbored evaporated when he heard Remy's last offer. She was too precious to be discarded, and the fact that Remy was willing to do so meant the man didn't appreciate what God had given him. He was saving Alara by eliminating Remy, and once he convinced her of the power of God's love, they would be able to convince many more, together, through the power of her angelic grace.

When enough bundles of newspapers were in the room to line the interior walls, Cortez began stacking more bundles around Remy. He didn't hear Remy's apologies, or tears; he was lost in daydreams of the future, when his role in the Church's salvation would be beyond question. He imagined all the eyes on him and Alara when he entered their place of worship, basking in the warmth of their gaze. His sudden shift from the shadows to the light, from staying hidden to being seen, was empowered by the strength of his love for Alara, the woman he was certain God had put on earth, in his path, for a reason. One small bump in the road remained, and he would soon be taken by hell's flames for his sins.

Cortez separated the newspapers at the top of the piles

surrounding Remy. The pages were thrown on the floor, some crumpled, some floating through the air on unseen breezes, until the floor was covered in gray and black. As he worked, Cortez would find an eye-catching headline, then read it aloud to Remy.

"Five dead in terrorist attack."

"Cowboys are Super Bowl champions!"

"Markets recover after days of turmoil."

Remy waited for the end with the smell of chicken tortilla soup and the morning newspaper in his nostrils. For some reason, the scent reminded him of his father. He wished he could tell him goodbye, thank him for sticking around, and ask him if he'd ever regretted being a father in the first place. When it was clear that Cortez was pleased with his preparation, Remy began praying, talking to a God he had never known but hoped would still listen.

A description of the liberation of Buchenwald by American forces played on the screen behind Cortez when he pulled out the lighter. He pulled a *Money* magazine from his back pocket.

"I saw this on the shelf and thought it was perfect," he said with his childlike voice filled with innocence.

Remy recognized the cover; it was a subscription his father had kept for years. "I'm sorry," Remy said. Not to Cortez, but to his father—an apology for leaving his family behind without an explanation.

Cortez sparked the flame and held it to the corner of the magazine. It wouldn't light. He tried different edges, different corners; none of them worked.

Inspired by the Holy Spirit, Cortez brought the lighter to his face, breathed on it, then kissed it before lighting it again. He held the flame to the magazine and it erupted into flame, the dry sheets of paper accepting the heat like a thirsty traveler in the desert.

Remy and Cortez met eyes with the flames between them. Remy dropped his gaze and let his chin rest against his chest. Seeing this gesture of defeat, Cortez stood tall, took a deep breath, and dropped the magazine. He walked out, closing the door on the growing inferno.

# CHAPTER TWENTY-ONE

THE SUPERVISOR SENSED Alara's purpose for checking the time and reminded her of how much time remained before she could leave. For him, these were precious moments, ones he wouldn't release from his vice grip, even under the most pressing instances, because he held the strictest certainty that once she left the premises she was beyond his reach; he would have to cross another chasm of time before another scheduled shift together.

Alara went back to the line of waiting drinks with renewed determination to find the end. The customers that day had never seen, and never saw again, someone work with her haunted intensity of a madwoman, her insides aflame with the knowledge of the burning books. Pots of steamed milk and shots of espresso were pulled from thin air, as if there were twice as many machines and baristas operating them, and the entire operation took on the cool efficiency of a special forces mission. With the line of drinks eradicated, and before more could be added, she cleaned the floors, wiped the tables, and stocked the sugar packets customers used for black coffee. While Alara was in the lobby, her specter started the production process when a new customer placed their order, replaced by her physical form when the time came to hand off the drinks, so the waiting customers wouldn't have their corporeal sensibilities offended by her spirit.

By ten minutes after the call, Alara had taken care of behind the counter as well: the cups were stocked, syrups replaced, counters cleaned, and new milks behind old in the refrigerator. She swept and mopped the floor where the employees stood without any of her coworkers taking a single step from their positions. In short, there was no work left for the other employees before closing, other than taking care of the customers, and she told the supervisor as much when she requested to leave early, her myriad tasks completed.

The supervisor licked his lips. Beads of sweat glistened on his forehead. "You've still got another half hour," he said.

Alara, staring at the sweaty face, became aware of her own perspiration. The rapid work had been difficult but wasn't responsible for her shirt sticking to her skin; her skin dripped from the effort required to be in two places at once.

"Come on, I've done everything," Alara said. She looked at him with the stare generations of beautiful women had perfected over years of bending men's iron will. "Can't you let me go, just this once? I never ask for anything." She blinked twice and softened her expression, accentuating her good looks.

The supervisor wasn't the type of man who shied away from the truth. He knew, without ever being told, that he had no shot with Alara. Her feminine charms had the opposite effect on the possessive supervisor: his heart hardened with a fierce determination to wring every second of her presence from her that he could. Being a practical man as well, and lazy, he also enjoyed the work she had saved him from, and he grew inspired to squeeze still more from his desperate employee.

"The bathrooms still aren't done," he said with a sadistic

smile. The thought of degrading Alara by having her clean the bathrooms he himself frequented did more to awaken his slumbering genitals than any of her curves.

Alara didn't wait for a promise, or for a direct request. Leaving her ghost making drinks at the counter, she took the mop, the window cleaner, the toilet cleaner, and the disinfectant and proceeded to make quick work of the bathrooms. When she returned to the employees' side of the counter, she found six drinks waiting to be handed off. She washed her hands before giving the drinks to the waiting customers, who would have rushed out if they were handed drinks from anything but a flesh-and-blood human. She checked the clock and found that there were still twenty-five minutes remaining in her shift.

At that exact moment, unknown to her, Cortez was struggling to light the magazine. The fire hadn't started, yet, but she imagined thousands of unknown pages throwing inked ash into the air and couldn't bear another moment away from the blaze. The flurry of work helped her escape the gravity of the situation, but without any tasks left, her thoughts had nowhere to hide. Her stomach twisted like a slug sprinkled with salt.

She took off her apron and went into the back room to clock out. The supervisor, his hungry eyes always watching, blocked her path back to the lobby with his enormous frame.

"Where do you think you're going? I didn't say you could leave."

"I did the bathrooms," Alara said, exasperated. She stared at him. "I need to go. Fire me if you want."

The supervisor said, "I will!" the way a child might claim he would stay awake until midnight on New Year's Eve.

Alara knew he would fall asleep well before the ball dropped. "OK, I'll worry about that when it happens," she said. She grabbed her purse, flung it over her shoulder, and tried to walk out.

The supervisor didn't move. Still acting a child, he didn't recognize the ramifications his continued overbearing behavior could produce on his career, instead believing it was his divine right to rule, and his subject's subservience had been decreed by a higher authority.

Alara tried to squeeze past but he blocked her with the bulk of his frame. She stood back, frustrated, and he smiled with delight.

The employee at the register, the sole person dealing with customers, yelled to them, saying one of them needed to come make drinks.

The supervisor's beady eyes focused on Alara, his heavy eyebrows cinched together. "That's all you," he said.

Alara took a deep breath. She had better things to do than argue with a child. Books were burning, and while there was nothing she could do to stop the conflagration, she at least wanted to be there to pay her respects.

The emergency door in the back room had a bright red handle with numerous warnings about the attached alarm. The entire store would hear, customers included, and disturbing Decant's operations would harm her chances of continued employment more than upsetting a supervisor nobody liked. Left with no other options, she turned around and walked towards it.

When the supervisor realized the lengths she was willing to traverse in order to leave, and knowing the store's manager would hear about the alarm, the supervisor told Alara to wait.

Alara turned around with one hand on the handle and glared at the sweating supervisor.

"Don't! You can leave this way," he said, moving out of the way and holding out an arm, courtesy replacing obstinacy.

"Too late," Alara said. A blaring siren erupted overhead at the exact moment she pushed the bright red handle, accompanied by flashing white lights feared by epileptics. She drank in the chaos of the scene inside Decant, the stunned faces of the supervisor and her coworker in the store's main area, then turned, letting the door close under its own weight, and headed to the library.

SHE TRIED CALLING Remy as soon as she left Decant. It went straight to voicemail. Her own memories of the library weighed heavily on her mind as she walked as fast as she could to its location, just short of breaking into a jog. Her father—an immigrant who'd had trouble reading himself but was convinced of the written word's power—had taken her to the city's library on Saturdays when she was young, walking hand in hand with her through the aisles while she chose three books for the week. Over the years, that number had grown to four, then four to five. There were many weeks she selected more than her allotment, but her father was adamant about the predetermined number, her first lesson in not receiving everything that she wanted.

If the crowd ahead hadn't been stopped on the corner, waiting to cross, she would have kept walking through the intersection without pause, lost in her memories.

The number of books she read had dwindled once she hit puberty and realized attention from boys could be just as enthralling and required little work on her part. Her pleasure reading ground to a halt during high school, when her scholastic demands combined with her social life to sap every ounce of free time from her life, often taking time away from her sleep as well. She received books as birthday presents each year, gifts she requested, and she added them to her collection, deliberating their placement on her shelf with care, with every intention of reading them as soon as time permitted.

Alara didn't see the automatic doors of the grocery store on her right open wide, and she almost ran headfirst into a woman with a load of groceries in each hand rushing out to a waiting car with its hazards on.

"Watch where you're going!" the woman yelled, the effort further straining her laboring body.

"Sorry," Alara said.

Reading time hadn't materialized until she moved out of her parents' house after graduating from high school. She never second-guessed her decision to bring her piles of books into the city with her, even while carrying the heavy boxes up three flights of stairs. Without her parents' expectation that she read, and subsequent disappointment, she rediscovered her passion for reading and began working through the volumes she'd collected over the years. Dating Remy provided her with a reason for ignoring men, which provided her still more time to catch up on years of neglected words.

Cortez assumed that Alara would care about the burning library because she loved reading books. He was wrong. Alara cared about the burning books because the library was the one place where her father had been proud of her, pride that was replaced by a creeping disappointment that spoiled their inter-actions during her teenage years.

Smoke rose between distant buildings. Alara quickened her pace, the fire's evidence extracting her from swirling memories. One lingering question remained, a small sliver of a fact that stuck to the back of her skull like gum on a shoe: How had Remy known about the library fire?

Alara was among the first people standing transfixed outside the library. She stood in the building's shadow, staring up at the smoke, wondering how much damage the stone building would suffer. Someone bumped into her while her eyes were skyward, yelling that she should keep moving as they strode past. Words escaped her when she attempted a reply, incinerated as they rose from her stomach to her throat. The overwhelming desire to be alone took hold of her and wouldn't let go. Though her soul wanted to witness the fire and luxuriate in the resultant pain, her body was called to escape to the park, to the trees, and to her bench. Her mind, the arbiter between her body's two forces, put forth a compromise, and so she relocated to the park opposite the library's front doors to watch the destruction unfold.

The crowds outside the library grew piecemeal. Most people took one look at the smoke issuing from the library's roof and hurried past, or crossed the street and hurried past, certain that their destination was more important than the fire. The drivers, after seeing onlookers staring into the sky from the side-walk, leaned low so they could see the building's top—none of them stopped. The people who congregated outside the library, the ones who couldn't ignore the destruction, stood in solemn reverence of knowledge's cremation. They each wanted to scream at the people who passed, to question them about what was worth stopping for, if not the burning of something as pure as books.

Alara wondered if any of the books her fingers had touched were already gone. It had been so long since she'd been in the library that she couldn't remember if the children's books, the ones she devoured with the tenacity of a dog with a bone, were on the bottom levels or were closer to the top, where the thickest smoke issued from the building. She shook her head at her false assumption, that the books on top were the ones burning, knowing that smoke rises and therefore the books on the bottom floor could just as well be on fire and the smoke would still appear in the same location.

. . .

CORTEZ CHOSE that moment to leave the side of the building, where he had been watching Alara from a distance, and approach his beloved. He did his best to stand tall despite the shooting pain every breath produced in his aching ribs, walking forward with the certainty that everyone watching the fire was also aware of his holy steps. He'd had enough of hiding in the shadows and was glad to have an audience. They would soon get to see what he was prepared to do for Alara's love.

Alara didn't notice the broken man scuttling across the street from the library until it became obvious she was his destination. His shirt was torn on his leaning torso, which was misshapen from favoring one side of his rib cage. She recognized Cortez out of the corner of her eye while still staring in horror at the smoke issuing from the roof of the library. Dealing with him was the last thing she wanted while the pages inside were burning. She prepared herself for his arrival by imagining she had a twin and swapping places with her counterpart, a useful strategy for ignoring men she had often employed in the past whenever one of their ranks grew too familiar for her taste.

Cortez walked right up to her and stopped mere steps away. His ravenous eyes sparkled with a newfound confidence, a mania Alara sensed without seeing his face. She looked at him, pretending not to know who he was. When it became obvious he wouldn't be deterred, she lit the lighthouse of recognition hidden behind her eyes.

"What are you doing here?" she said, annoyed.

"The library's burning," he said. He didn't elaborate.

"I can't believe it," Alara said, filling the silence. She continued staring at the library, and Cortez continued staring at her, unwilling to peel his eyes away from her beauty and look in the direction of her gaze.

He turned around at the arrival of the first fire truck; its siren cut off as it pulled to a stop in front of the library. Its chipped paint and rusted ladder matched the firefighters who trickled out with aged equipment that had seen better days. A moment later, two more fire trucks, newer than the first, screamed around the corner and skidded to a stop. Without hesitation, a driver of one of the newer trucks told the first truck to move. With the space occupied by the first cleared, the two trucks positioned themselves in front of the library's wide steps with the older truck behind.

The street in front of the library transformed into a hive of activity. The road running between the library and the park was closed off, forcing cars to stop. Some drivers climbed out of their cars, watching the unfolding attempts to save the library, and others turned down side streets, frustrated and searching for a way around.

"Remy's in there," Cortez said.

Alara looked at Cortez in disbelief, studying his face, searching for hints of a lie. Cortez didn't waver in his certainty. Her boyfriend, the notorious nonreader, was in the library; she couldn't piece together a single reason why. "Remy?" she said.

"Uh huh," Cortez said, his voice suffused with laughter that didn't transfer onto his face. This confirmation was said in the same manner as a child who knows the end of a picture book but doesn't want to share the knowledge with the adult they are reading it with for the first time—it was a joke to him.

Despite her disgust at Cortez's delivery, Alara weighed the information. There was still a chance her boyfriend was alive. In that moment, she forgot about her recent displeasure with him, ignored the alleged time spent with other women, and wanted him out of the fire, safe by her side. "What's he doing in there?" she said. "How do you know?" Turning away from Cortez, she looked for the closest firefighter, deciding between reporting his presence in the fire to the worn-out firefighters from the first truck or telling the haughty, gleaming men who'd arrived in the second wave.

"Relax," Cortez said, stretching out the word. "There's nothing to worry about. God brought me here for a reason."

Alara would've expected Cortez's tone if she were badgering him about leaving for the airport earlier than necessary; in their current situation, his delivery was cold, detached. Alara didn't put any stock into his proclamation. She imagined this was yet another childlike fantasy, and she cursed the men in her life who refused to grow up. In that instant, and for the first time, she realized why she was drawn to Remy, alongside numerous other women: he acted like a grown man.

"Of course there's something to worry about! Remy's inside a fire!" she said, her words erupting on Cortez. She hoped her urgency would pull Cortez from his uncaring attitude.

Cortez looked around at the people watching the library fire, the ones who were about to witness his sacrifice. With a nonchalant air, he informed her that he could save him.

"And what are you going to do?" she snapped.

Cortez looked at Alara with a heart full of love and an overwhelming sense of larger purpose. This was the moment he had been waiting for, his chance to prove to her, and everyone around, that he was a great man destined for great things. It was the first step in his ascendancy, the domino to begin a cascade of events that would result in Alara by his side at church.

"I'll go in and get him," Cortez replied. A great weight evaporated from his shoulders now that his body was on the line, filling him with lightness. He imagined Jesus felt the same way after refusing to defend himself before Pilate.

# CHAPTER TWENTY-TWO

CORTEZ STOOD on the sidewalk between Alara and the library. She moved him to the side with the back of her hand and proceeded to walk towards the firefighters, determined to report her boyfriend's presence in the fire. It was her duty to tell a professional about the potential victim, something Cortez should have done himself. She knew Remy was Cortez's perceived obstacle to her, so it came as no surprise her stalker would leave her boyfriend to his fate, but she second-guessed both his knowledge and his intentions. The absolute certainty encapsulated in Cortez's words sent chills down her spine. How did he know beyond a shadow of a doubt?

Alara's myriad thoughts ran on parallel tracks in her knotted stomach and her aching heart. They arose as a sudden awareness, with little processing required, and emerged in their final form before she took two steps. She was stopped by Cortez's firm hold on her arm before she could step down from the sidewalk and onto the street.

"I'll be right back," Cortez said. He waited a breath for a response, and upon receiving none, listened to his body's urges to touch her. He reached an arm up and brushed her cheek with the back of his hand, certain this was the part of the movie when the woman realized the identity of the man destiny had decided should be hers.

The library's collapsing floor created a loud crashing noise that blanketed the streets; Cortez's delusion continued, self-propagating. Alara, frozen, couldn't find the strength to pull away. At last, Cortez knew the time was right to put his plan into action.

He positioned himself between Alara and the library then took two steps backwards, still staring at Alara, drinking in the angel placed on earth for him with his eyes, and said, swelling with pride, "If God has put me in a position to help, I can't look the other way."

With his final words, Cortez turned around and ran past the worn fire truck, then between the two new ones. The firefighters, still close to the trucks and wearing their heavy gear, tried stopping him. One managed to grab a hold of his shirt but the garment ripped further, exposing all of Cortez's chest. Past the barriers, he bounded up the wide stone steps two at a time, ignoring his aversion to the front door, in full view of the trees, because there wasn't time to run around the entire building. Cortez ignored another crash that issued from inside the library; nothing would stop him from completing his holy mission. He was a man possessed by a power greater than himself, and he rushed into the library as the inferno raged overhead.

A MOMENTARY AWARENESS of a memory that didn't belong to her, a mere flash of a vision, transported Alara through time. Her father had mentioned his family's history many times, under many circumstances, and the legend of her ancestors—which had influenced her opinion of organized religion, in particular Catholicism—appeared to Alara as she watched the growing fire. He'd told her all about the clergy burning the Mayan-language books in the 1500s, urging her to remember so she could one day pass the knowledge on to her own children. There were people in Mexico who could still trace the date based on the Mayan calendar, so he claimed, and he made her promise she'd remember to do her part to preserve the memory, saying their culture had been taken from them and that one day they'd have their revenge against the priest who'd instigated the destruction.

While fire truck sirens pierced the air in the distance, growing louder as they sped through the city streets, Alara stood beneath the trees in the park, staring without seeing at the base of the library, trying to preserve what she saw in her vision. She was in another place, at another time, staring out from among the trees, watching a circle of men dressed in brown habits, holding thick wooden clubs, surrounding a fire. Behind the men was a raised wooden platform with a man seated in the center, his face obscured by shadow. Next to the platform, also protected by the club-wielding men, was a series of wooden structures supporting men hanging from tied hands—men she sensed she knew. Without introspection, Alara knew her grief came from both the men and the fire. It was the burning books of the Mayan people, the flames her father had urged her to commit to memory until the day she died, and the hanging men were her ancestors.

Raising her gaze and watching the smoke, Alara couldn't help but think that the people of the city deserved to lose their culture in the same way her ancestors had centuries ago. The library fire wasn't the punishment they deserved, because no fire would ever be enough—all the books that would burn in the library fire could, and would, be replaced. There was no one to replace the tomes her ancestors wrote, nobody to print another edition; they were lost to time, erased from human history by a priest who'd decided the power for his judgment had been bestowed upon him by God.

SWINGING open the library's massive wooden doors released a wave of heat that dried Cortez's mouth and singed his hair. The noise was deafening, the roar from a waterfall of flames. He smiled as he stormed over the threshold. The belief that Alara would recognize what he had done for her, the beginning of their future together, created enough euphoria for him to face down the fires of hell if required by fate.

Thick black smoke, pungent with the smell of burning paper and ink, obscured the top of the grand staircase on the far side of the lobby. Cortez experienced a momentary pang of guilt for lying to Alara—Remy was dead on the top floor. He remembered his mother's words, that a man's soul is safe as long as he goes to church each week and confesses. Nothing would keep him from attending church the upcoming Sunday. There was a lot the Lord needed to hear.

Cortez couldn't wait to see the look on Alara's face when she discovered he had saved her favorite book. It had been his plan all along: get rid of Remy and impress her by emerging from the fire with *Love in the Time of Cholera* safe and sound, held high in victory. Even if she needed time after losing Remy —time Cortez would give her—she wouldn't be able to deny Cortez's value, evidenced by his grand gesture. In the end, she would be his.

The heat and smoke in the lobby obscured his vision, and Cortez relied on the knowledge of previous excursions to navigate through slitted eyes. He ran past the main staircase and into the stacks on the first floor. The books were all still intact, untouched by flame, but the overwhelming heat meant combustion could occur at any moment. Cortez's eyes watered from the smoke, moisture that evaporated as soon as it hit his cheeks. Even squinting was difficult. He turned right and closed his eyes, running down the length of the wall, his hands guiding his path. He stopped when his breathing became heavy then looked around through narrowed eyes, trying to get his bearings.

If he could find the smaller staircase that led to the second floor, he could dart into the black smoke to where Alara's gift waited for him.

Knowing he was close, Cortez closed his eyes again and ran through a row of books, crossing to the other side of the first floor. His right hand located the end of the bookshelf he ran along, and he shot out his left hand to find the book-covered wall across the aisle. He dared another peek and found the staircase in its expected location.

Cortez crawled on hands and knees up the stairs. The smoke was stifling, the heat oppressive, and the noise of the fire was magnified, no longer muffled by the ceiling. He lifted the bottom of his torn shirt up to protect his face, taking deep breaths through the fabric. His ordeal was almost complete. He crawled forward with an awkward three-limbed stance, one hand reserved for keeping the shirt over his mouth. When he thought he'd gone far enough and was at the correct bookshelf, he used the shelves to hoist himself to standing. Finding the book he'd left behind, he then crouched back down, inspecting the title.

It wasn't the right book. He had grabbed *The Universe in a Nutshell*.

Cortez groaned. His head started to ache as the power bestowed upon him by the thought of a future with Alara receded into the past, and his senses started fading from the lack of oxygen. He stood once more, grabbed another title, and didn't need to read the title to know it wasn't the correct book. On the third try, he attempted to open his eyes while standing. He couldn't register a single title in front of his face through the smoke.

In a rage fueled by inadequacy, he swiped the entire shelf of books down. Lowering himself to the ground, he felt for books that were the correct size, the right thickness, and when he found a candidate, he forced his screaming eyes to open, making them scan the cover.

None of the books were the one he was looking for.

Some of the books had fallen further into the stacks when they were tossed from their shelf. The third and fourth floors had collapsed onto the second floor, scattering debris among the shelves that filled the spaces where Cortez searched. Cortez crawled into the mire, his hands leading him along trails of pages that would soon be incinerated. Growing desperate, he scanned cover after cover, searching, despite the searing pain in his eyes. He spun around when he felt more books under his feet, then spun again when his movements knocked more books down from their shelves. All the while, the fire raged above him, around him, licking the room's walls and approaching his position from above.

Still without the book he came for, he felt himself suffocating and panicked. It had never occurred to him that the fire he'd started out of love would ever turn against him. He turned, looking for the staircase, and felt himself kick one final book, lying atop charred remains. The feeling reverberated through his bones, sending a shock of recognition through every nerve in his body. Ignoring his suffering lungs and blistering skin, he crawled to the book, the farthest one from freedom. He lowered himself when both hands were over the book's assumed location, sunken in the debris. Prone against the floor, he opened his eyes as best he could. Through his squint, he saw it: *Love in the Time of Cholera*. With renewed drive, he grabbed the book with his left hand and tried turning back to the staircase.

He was stuck, his right arm trapped.

Cortez, frantic once more, leaned close to his arm, inspecting what held it fast. His hand was trapped inside a rib cage, Remy's rib cage, and the skeleton wouldn't move. He twisted and turned his arm, believing the man he'd sentenced to death had escaped from the room and was now returning the favor by making sure Cortez was incinerated alongside him. Cortez, now on his knees, pulled and pushed, straining so hard he thought he'd break bones, though the force he produced was nowhere near enough. His vision narrowed, and through smoke he saw the skull, its jaws open. Laughter surrounded him; farther away, tortured screams. Terrified, Cortez poured every ounce of strength into a final pull.

It was enough to send him bowling back. He collapsed onto his back, still holding the book tightly against his chest. Sputtering, he turned over and found his right hand carried extra weight—the rib cage, detached from the skeleton. With his eyes closed, he crawled in the darkness, one slow elbow at a time through the deafening whoosh of consumed air, in the direction he believed was the staircase that would lead to his salvation. The noise of the vortex produced by the hungry flames soon faded away, leaving him senseless while he wormed along the second-level floor.

Cortez never arrived at the staircase. His last crawl didn't have enough strength behind it to move him forward, and he lay down with Alara's favorite book beneath him, a thin smile on his blistered lips from the knowledge that he had died for love.

ALARA HAD RECOVERED control of her body as soon as Cortez ran into the library. She rushed forward, following in his footsteps, until she got to the firefighters, their backs turned around as they watched the crazed Cortez running into the flames.

"You have to help my boyfriend! He's inside!" Alara said.

"That nut was your boyfriend?" a firefighter responded when he saw her.

"We saw. He ran right past us," his comrade added.

"No, he's not my boyfriend. There's another guy in there!"

"Look, there's nothing we can do. They're in charge now." The two firefighters, both from the first truck, spit on the ground at the mention of the men who had taken their place in front of the blaze and forced them to the rear.

Alara ran forward. Before she could utter a word, the firefighter holding the hose told her to stand back.

"My boyfriend is in there!" she yelled over the combined noise of the fire, water, and general pandemonium.

"There's nothing we can do until we get the blaze under control. Stand back!"

Alara looked around, unsure. Reality was slipping away from her, the world a blur as if she were spinning around when, in fact, she was standing still. Two lingering questions remained, sticking into her like hooks and refusing to let go.

Why was Remy inside the library?

How did Cortez know?

Stumbling back beneath the trees, she sat down with her back resting on a trunk, her elbows on her knees, head buried in her arms. When she called Remy's phone it went straight to voicemail again. She tossed the phone back into her purse and cursed Cortez, the one person who might have the answers, for running back into the blaze. His words echoed in her head, his declaration that God had put him in a position to help, and an ancient anger rose up in her. In an inspired flash of understanding, she knew Cortez's face belonged to the man seated on the wooden platform presiding over the conflagration in her vision, the one hidden in shadow. He was responsible for the burning books of her people, he was responsible for the burning books in the library, and without being told, she knew he was responsible for Remy's presence in the flames.

Even with this knowledge, she couldn't wish him dead. Death was too quick an exit. He had to suffer, to hurt, to beg for his life in exchange for what he'd done to her ancestors. Her own loss of her boyfriend was minuscule compared to the generations of suffering caused by his actions.

The minutes dragged by. Curious onlookers came and went, staying for various lengths of time, as night descended on the city. Few stayed until the blaze was under control, and fewer still stayed once the firefighters entered the burned building, searching for survivors. At some point, portable lights were brought, illuminating the fire trucks and the area in front of the library. Bugs flew around the bulbs, calling out to their brethren to come forth from the park into the continuation of the daylight. Their counterparts in the park responded, creating a cacophony of buzzing wings and various clicks, pops, and whirls.

Alara stood up when the first firefighters entered the building. She didn't have to wait long until they came out nodding their heads, indicating no survivors had been found. The rescuers went in a second time, returning minutes later. They grabbed a stretcher then rushed back inside. After tense minutes that crawled past like hours, the firefighters reemerged with a charred and blistered body covered with a white sheet. Alara ran forward, taking stock of the size of the remains, wondering if she could tell the difference between the shape of Remy's body and Cortez's.

"Can't come over here," a firefighter said, holding a hand up to her. Behind him, one of the men told the other how the body they'd recovered was holding a book. "Guess he was trying to save this one from being burned," he said, holding the book up. It was charred but intact.

"Did you find any other bodies nearby?" Alara called out, her voice betraying her anxiety. She wanted to know if Cortez had even made it to Remy in the first place, thinking the two of them might have been caught while they were exiting the blaze.

"Nope, just a bunch of books. His hand was caught in part of a bookshelf," the firefighter responded without a second thought.

"Which book was it?" Alara asked. It was an odd question.

The man looked at her, then looked at one of his comrades. The comrade shrugged. The man with knowledge of the book looked back at Alara, then told her it was the Bible.

"It was burned too," he added.

Alara knew it was Cortez. She guessed that when he realized he wouldn't make it out alive he'd clung to his faith like a life preserver, hoping his God would save him from the flames.

"Good," she said.

The book crumbled in the firefighter's hand. Cortez had run into the flames but hadn't been able to save the sacred text.

# COULD YOU DO ME A FAVOR?

Please help other readers learn more about this book by leaving a rating and review!

Then head over to my website authormarcoshernandez.com and subscribe to my email list. You'll hear about upcoming releases and deals you don't want to miss!

ALSO BY MARCOS ANTONIO HERNANDEZ

Android City Chronicles

The Return of the Operator

Before Anyone Finds Out

Good Enough in a Pinch

———

The Edited Genome Trilogy

Awakening

Alternative

Absolution

———

Hispanic American Heritage Stories

The Education of a Wetback

Where They Burn Books

They Also Burn People

Demons in the Golden Empire

———

Indigenous Magic

Jesus Chan and the Return of Mayan Magic

## ABOUT THE AUTHOR

Marcos Antonio Hernandez writes from the suburbs of Washington, D.C. An avid reader of both fiction and non-fiction, his favorite authors are Haruki Murakami and Philip K. Dick — in that order.

Marcos graduated from the University of Maryland, College Park with a degree in chemical engineering and a minor in physics. Since graduating, he has worked as a barista, a food scientist, and a CrossFit coach.

*They Also Burn People* is Marcos's eighth novel.

authormarcoshernandez.com

Made in the USA
Columbia, SC
26 September 2023